FAMILY

CHILDHOOD MEMORIES
AND OTHER STORIES

CHILDHOOD MEMORIES
AND OTHER STORIES

Giuseppe Tomasi di Lampedusa

Translated by Stephen Parkin

Foreword by Ian Thomson

Edited by Gioacchino Lanza Tomasi
and Alessandro Gallenzi

ALMA CLASSICS

ALMA CLASSICS
an imprint of

ALMA BOOKS LTD
London House
243–253 Lower Mortlake Road
Richmond
Surrey TW9 2LL
United Kingdom
www.almaclassics.com

First published as *I racconti* in November 1961 by Giangiacomo Feltrinelli
Editore, Milan, Italy
This translation first published by Alma Classics in 2013
© Giangiacomo Feltrinelli Editore, 1961
Translation © Stephen Parkin, 2013
Foreword © Ian Thomson, 2013
Notes © Alma Classics, 2013
Biographical Note © Gioacchino Lanza Tomasi

Supported using public funding by
**ARTS COUNCIL
ENGLAND**
LOTTERY FUNDED

Printed and bound by CPI Group (UK) Ltd, Croydon, CR0 4YY

ISBN: 978-1-84749-305-7
eBook ISBN: 978-1-84749-339-2

Contents

Foreword by Ian Thomson   VII
Note on the Texts   XIV

Childhood Memories   I
Joy and the Law   73
The Siren   83
The Blind Kittens   127

Notes   153
Biographical Note   177

Giuseppe Tomasi di Lampedusa in the
drawing room of Villa Piccolo in 1955

Lampedusa's most illustrious
Tomasi ancestor, Ferdinando II Maria
(1697–1775)

Niccolò I Filangeri,
7th Prince of Cutò
(1760–1839)

Alessandro IV Filangeri, Lampedusa's
maternal great-grandfather
(1802–54)

Teresa Merli Clerici, Lampedusa's
maternal great-grandmother
(1816–97)

Giulio Fabrizio Tomasi, Lampedusa's paternal great-grandfather,
on which the character of Don Fabrizio in *The Leopard* is based
(1815–85)

Giuseppe Tomasi, Lampedusa's
paternal grandfather
(1838–1908)

Stefania Papè e Vanni,
Lampedusa's paternal grandmother
(1840–1913)

Lucio Mastrogiovanni Tasca,
Lampedusa's maternal grandfather
(1842–1918)

Giovanna Filangeri di Cutò,
Lampedusa's maternal grandmother
(1850–91)

Lampedusa's mother, Beatrice Mastrogiovanni Tasca di Cutò (1870–1946, left)
and the "godlike beauty" Franca Florio (1873–1950, right)

Beatrice Cutò and Franca Florio on a boat off the coast
of Favignana in the summer of 1902

Giuseppe Tomasi
at the age of five
wearing a uniform

Giuseppe Tomasi in the
gardens of the Palazzo Filangeri Cutò
in Santa Margherita Belice

Another picture of Giuseppe Tomasi in the gardens
of the Palazzo Filangeri Cutò. In the background,
his parents Giulio and Beatrice

The Palazzo Filangeri di Cutò in Santa Margherita Belice
and the "Chiesa Madre" in a photograph from the 1950s,
before they were destroyed by an earthquake

The "grand staircase" in the second
courtyard leading to the main entrance
gate of the Palazzo Filangeri di Cutò

A detail from the "grand banquet"
painting in the dining room of the Palazzo
Filangeri di Cutò

Don Onofrio Rotolo,
the caretaker of the Palazzo
Filangeri di Cutò

The "curious oval copper bathtub"
in which Lampedusa "was made to have a bath"
when he was a child

The leopard in an eighteenth-
century coat of arms

The coat of arms of the Filangeri
di Cutò family

The Venaria hunting lodge, built in the eighteenth century by
Alessandro II Filangeri and destroyed by the
1968 Belice earthquake

A group of *campieri* of the Filangeri estate
at the Venaria hunting lodge.

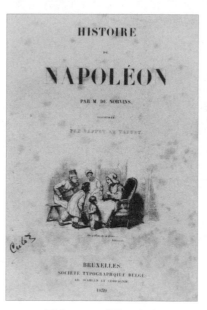

Title page of Norvins's
Histoire de Napoléon,
first published in 1827

Alessandra Wolff Stomersee ("Licy"),
Lampedusa's wife
(1894–1982)

Pietro Tomasi della Torretta,
Lampedusa's uncle
(1873–1962)

Alice Wolff, née Barbi, wife of
Pietro Tomasi and mother of Licy
(1858–1948)

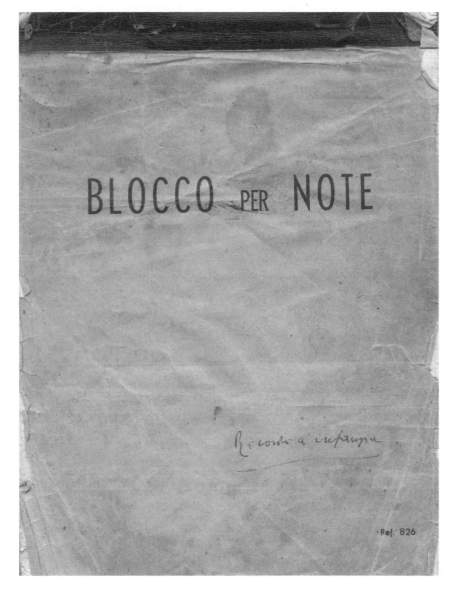

The cover of the notebook in which Lampedusa
wrote his 'Childhood Memories'

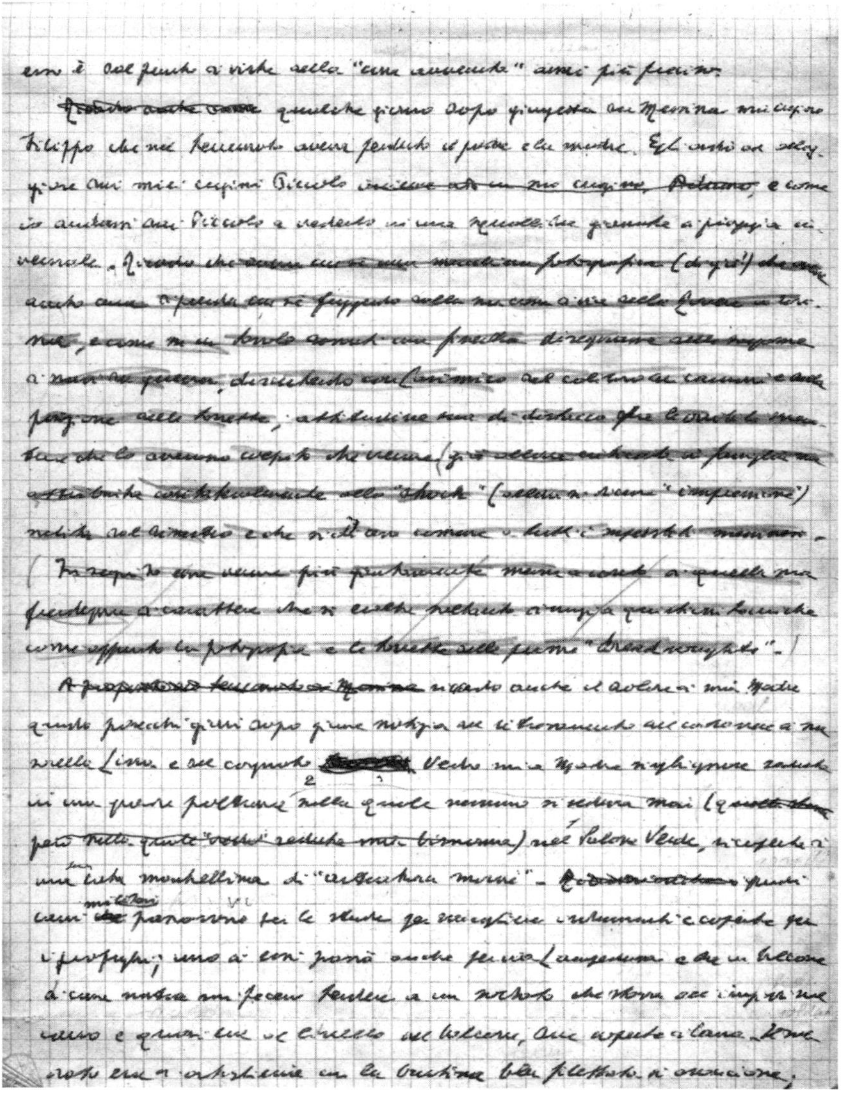

A manuscript page from 'Childhood Memories'

Foreword

Published posthumously in 1958, *The Leopard* is a classic of Italian literature embroidered with reflections on dynastic power and Sicily's age-old burden of injustice and death. The novel chronicles the demise of the Sicilian aristocracy on the eve of the unification of Italy in 1860, and the emergence of a bourgeois class that would evolve into the Mafia.

Giuseppe Tomasi di Lampedusa, a lifelong smoker, died of lung cancer a year before his novel appeared in Italy in 1958. So he was spared knowledge of the controversy it would provoke. The paradox expressed at the heart of *The Leopard* – that "everything must change, so that nothing has to change" – was interpreted by left-leaning critics as a cynical defence of Sicilian conservatism and Sicilian fatalism. The novel was reckoned crushingly old-fashioned – a "success for the Right", Alberto Moravia complained – as well as ideologically unsound.

Italian publishers rejected the manuscript until it found a home with Feltrinelli Editore in Milan (ironically a *gauchiste* company). Lampedusa was in some ways a deep-dyed conservative and not at first averse to Italian Fascism. "Even if a revolution breaks out," he wrote from Paris in 1925, "no one will touch a hair on my head or steal one penny from me because by my side I have... Mussolini!" The youthful Lampedusa saw in the cult of *ducismo* a robust alternative to parliamentary liberalism; indeed, the Duce's attempts to uproot the Mafia were applauded by many Sicilians.

Later, however, Lampedusa became wholly indifferent to Fascism. Political enthusiasm of any sort was tiresome to him; he scorned liberals and monarchists alike. Born a prince, he lived as a prince, and put something of his own personality into *The Leopard*'s fictional Don Fabrizio Corbera, Prince of Salina. Lost in a heat-ridden backwater of western Sicily, Don Fabrizio is the Leopard of the title, a sceptically inclined man drawn to astronomy and the lucid pleasures of abstract thought. Life in the Salina palace moves round him at a seignorial snail's pace; the extinction of his name and lineage is imminent.

The Leopard is, among other things, a meditation on mortality. "While there's death there's hope," says Don Fabrizio axiomatically. His personal tax collector Don Calogero Sedara, a money-grubbing arriviste with an eye on the Salina estates, is the personification of the new and dangerous middle class which sprung up in Sicily following the collapse of the Bourbon regime. The old privilege based on rank and lineage was about to give way to a new privilege based on capital and entrepreneurial cunning. The unstated theme of *The Leopard* is not just the death of an aristocracy or a redundant way of life, but more broadly of Sicily – and of Europe.

By the time Lampedusa died in Sicily at the age of sixty, the Mafia had pervaded entire patrician quarters of the capital of Palermo where he was born. Quick money was to be made out of the city's reconstruction in the wake of the Allied bombings of 1943. Wretchedly, the family's Palermitan residence of the Palazzo Lampedusa was destroyed and pillaged following an American aerial raid. For the rest of his life Lampedusa remained sunk in debt and helpless to resist the demise of his own class. Today the Lampedusa family line is extinct.

The novelist Giorgio Bassani, in his preface to the 1958 first edition of *The Leopard*, spoke of the existence of other writings by Lampedusa. Among these were letters, short stories and notes made by Lampedusa on French and English literature. It was Bassani's hope that one day these writings would be published. Unfortunately Lampedusa's widow, Alexandra Wolff Stomersee ("Licy"), had embargoed publication (as well as consultation) of most of the material. Described by some as a difficult, at times prickly woman, she had her own history of loss and sorrow to contend with. In 1939 Licy had been forced to flee her native Latvia ahead of Stalin's advancing Red Army, while the family estate of Stomersee near Riga was turned by the Soviets into an agricultural school.

Only on Licy's death in 1982 were efforts made to publish Lampedusa's archive in its entirety. The fictional works and fragment of autobiography included in this book had originally appeared in Italy in different form in 1961. Lampedusa's widow had rearranged some of the material and subjected it to deletions. The cuts were ostensibly made in the interest of tidiness and discretion, but the removal (for example) of amusing anecdotes was less easy to justify. Now at last the four works are properly restored in English, and in a fine new translation by Stephen Parkin.

'Childhood Memories', written in Palermo over the summer of 1955, provides a fascinating glimpse into the background of *The Leopard*. A Proustian elegy to a lost past, it commemorates two dynastic homes whose loss – the one bombed, the other sold – pained Lampedusa tremendously. In conjuring his childhood memories of the Palazzo Lampedusa (the model for the Villa Salina in *The Leopard*) the writer-prince performed an astonishing feat of recollection. Lampedusa only had his memory to go on – there were no other resources for him – yet the writing has an incisive photographic clarity. The ballrooms, balconies and his mother's boudoir with its walls of coloured silk are all exquisitely rendered.

Lampedusa's mother, Beatrice Filangeri di Cutò, seems to have been a fretful woman forever worrying about her son's whereabouts. His marriage to the Baltic-born baroness was a source of anxiety to her – and perhaps also to Lampedusa. "It would torture me to have to be contested between her and you," he wrote to his mother from Latvia on 29th August 1932, adding: "You are the two people I hold most dear in the world." In his mother's dressing room, amid the hairbrushes and violet-scented perfumes, Lampedusa as a boy had been pampered like a pasha. His relationship with his mother went beyond mere filial devotion.

'The Siren', an exquisite story of which Lampedusa was justly proud, reads like a caprice from the *Arabian Nights* overlaid with Hellenic myth. In Fascist-era Turin, a Sicilian professor confides to a young journalist his love for a silver-tailed siren. The siren is a marine temptress from the pages of Homer. "Sweets should taste of sugar and nothing else," the professor says, wary perhaps of his story's fragile, fine-spun strangeness. Written in 1956–57, 'The Siren' is the most elaborately wrought of Lampedusa's fictions. The writing is as languorous and melancholy-tinged as in *The Leopard*, particularly in the descriptions of Sicily's wine-dark sea and its Hellenic temple-city landscapes, yet it has a fabulous undertow not found elsewhere in Lampedusa.

'Joy and the Law', completed over Christmas 1956, could not be a more different fiction. It tells of a poor clerk and his family in Palermo, and their windfall gift of a giant panettone and what to do with it. Neo-realist in tone, the story bears the influence of the newsreel school of documentary *verismo* as exemplified by the cinema of De Sica and Rossellini.

Lampedusa's knowledge of European film and literature was wide-ranging. Before visiting England in 1926, he had read all of Shakespeare, and was surely one of the first

Italians to fathom the obscurities of James Joyce's *Ulysses*. English literature was by no means popular in Sicily (or, for that matter, in mainland Italy) prior to the Second World War. Yet it afforded Lampedusa an escape from the sorry reality, as he saw it, of the times. Among his English idols was the seventeenth-century scholar-sportsman Izaak Walton, whose humour and gift for understatement clearly appealed. ("Hitler and Mussolini," Lampedusa judged, "had obviously not read Izaak Walton.") In the republican Sicily of the postwar years, Lampedusa must have cut a strange and lonely figure. During the dead hours of the Palermo afternoons he liked to discuss literature in a café with a circle of adoring cousins. With his briefcase full of poetry and marzipan pastries, this portly, sallow man was an aristocratic survivor.

Even today, northern Italians speak of Sicily as an African darkness – the place where Europe finally ends. The Arabs invaded Sicily in the ninth century, leaving behind mosques and pink-domed cupolas, and many Sicilians have a tincture of ancestral Arab blood. The Saracen influence remains strongest in the Mafia-infiltrated west of the island, where the Lampedusa properties were situated and where the sirocco blows in hot from Africa. Sicily, Lampedusa believed, was an island wounded both by its climate and history. 'The Blind Kittens', the opening chapter of an unfinished novel he begun in March 1957, was to chart the rise in turn-of-the-century Sicily of the Ibba family, prototype

Mafiosi who covet aristocratic estates and extort loans. Sicily emerges here as a comfortless landscape sweltering under a near-African heat. The Sicilian tendency to violence (in Lampedusa's estimation) was aggravated by the island's grudging sun and arid geography. Others have divined an antique beauty in this part of the Mezzogiorno. In 1963 Luchino Visconti, impressed by *The Leopard*'s exploration of love and political ambition, turned the novel into a sumptuous film starring Burt Lancaster as the beleaguered Sicilian Prince. Lampedusa would have been astonished to find himself mirrored in Lancaster; but also, perhaps, vindicated. His work, a marvel of poise and the high classical style, is with us still.

– Ian Thomson

Note on the Texts

The four pieces included in this volume were first published in Italy by Giangiacomo Feltrinelli Editore in 1961,
edited and with a preface by Giorgio Bassani. The 1961
Italian edition was based on typescripts of texts dictated
by Lampedusa's widow, Alexandra Wolff Stomersee. The
only extant manuscripts are those of 'Childhood Memories'
(including the recently rediscovered piece 'Torretta') and
a fragment of a first draft of 'The Siren'. There is also a
tape recording of Lampedusa reading 'The Siren', covering
around eighty per cent of the story.

The four pieces were written in the following order:
'Childhood Memories' (summer 1955), 'Joy and the Law'
(autumn 1956), 'The Siren' (winter 1956–57), 'The Blind
Kittens' (winter-spring 1957).

The manuscript of 'Childhood Memories', consisting of a mid-sized notebook of squared paper, is in the
possession of Giuseppe Biancheri, son of Olga Wolff
Stomersee, Licy's sister. The text is often broken up by
blank sheets of paper and occasionally crossed out. Many
of these deletions are by the author himself, but some
are certainly by Licy. The struck-out text is indicated in
our edition in bold font, whenever it is legible.

The first complete and unexpurgated edition of the four pieces was published in the Meridiani edition of the works of Giuseppe Tomasi di Lampedusa (Milano: Mondadori, 2004), edited by Nicoletta Polo, with introductions to the various works by Gioacchino Lanza Tomasi. With only a few emendations (and the reinstatement of a struck-out sentence that had been overlooked) based on further consultation of the 'Childhood Memories' manuscript, these are the texts on which our translation is based. Gioacchino Lanza Tomasi's *Premessa* to the four pieces in the Meridiani edition (grouped under the collective title *I racconti*) provides a fascinating insight into the emotional and biographical background to these texts, as well as further details about their composition and their significance in relation to Lampedusa's *The Leopard*.

The notes to the present volume – the first complete and unexpurgated English edition of Lampedusa's uncollected fiction – have been prepared by Alessandro Gallenzi with the invaluable help of Gioacchino Lanza Tomasi.

Childhood Memories

INTRODUCTION

I have very recently (mid-June 1955) reread *Henri Brulard** for the first time since the long-gone year of 1922. At that time I was still obsessed by the ideas of "clear beauty" and "subjective interest", and I remember that I didn't like the book.

Now I am ready to agree with those who think it almost ranks as Stendhal's masterpiece. There is an immediacy of feeling, an evident sincerity and a wonderful determination to dig through the accumulated strata of memory in order to reach what lies beneath. And what lucidity of style! How many impressions stream by, quite ordinary and yet so precious!

I should like to try and achieve the same effect. I actually feel duty-bound to do so. When the decline of life has set in, it becomes imperative to gather up as much as we can all the sensations that have passed through this body of ours. If it's true that only a very few (Rousseau, Stendhal, Proust) can make a masterpiece of it, most people should at least be able to preserve, in this way, what would otherwise, without this slight effort, be lost for ever. Keeping a diary or writing one's memoirs when one has reached a certain age should be an obligation imposed on us by the State: the material which would then accumulate over three or four generations would have inestimable value: many of the psychological and historical problems afflicting humanity would be solved. All written memoirs, even those of seemingly insignificant people, are of outstanding social value and rich in colour.

The extraordinary fascination we feel for Defoe's novels lies in the fact that they are almost like diaries – quite brilliantly so, even though invented. Think, then, what genuine diaries would be like! Just imagine the real diary of some courtesan in Regency Paris, or the memoirs of Byron's valet during his period in Venice!

So I will try to follow as closely as possible the method adopted in *Henri Brulard* – even to the point of including "maps" of the main locations.

But where I part company with Stendhal is over the "quality" of the memories which are evoked. He looks back on his childhood as a time when he was subjected to tyranny and abuse. I see my childhood as a lost paradise. Everyone was kind to me, I was treated like a king. Even those who later became hostile to me were, when I was a child, *aux petits soins.**

Therefore, my readers – though there won't be any – can expect to be taken on a stroll through a now lost Garden of Eden. If they get bored, I don't really care.

I plan to divide these 'Memoirs' into three parts. The first part, 'Childhood', will describe the period of my life up to my going to secondary school. The second, 'Youth', will take

us up to 1925. The third, 'Maturity', will continue to the present time, which I regard as the beginning of my old age.

Memories of childhood – for everyone I think – consist in a series of visual impressions, many of them still sharply focused, but lacking any kind of temporal sequence. To write a chronology of one's childhood is, in my view, impossible: even with the best will in the world, the result would only be a false representation based on terrible anachronisms. I will therefore adopt the method of grouping memories by topic, and in this way give an overall idea of them through spatial ordering rather than temporal succession. I will speak of the places where my childhood was spent, of the people who surrounded me and of my feelings (whose development I will not necessarily seek to trace).

I undertake to say nothing which is untrue. But I do not wish to write down *everything*: I reserve the right to lie by omission.

Unless I change my mind, of course.

MEMORIES

One of the earliest memories I can date with some precision, as it involves a verifiable historical event, goes back to 30th July 1900, when I was just a few days older than three and a half.*

I was with my mother* and her maid (probably Teresa, from Turin) in her dressing room. This room was longer than it was wide and was lit by a balcony at each of the short ends: one of them looked out onto the tiny garden separating our house from the Oratory of Santa Zita and the other onto a small internal courtyard. The bean-shaped (⌒) dressing table had a glass-covered surface, under which there was a pink fabric and legs covered in a sort of white-lace skirt. It was placed in front of the balcony that looked onto the garden. On it, there were hairbrushes and other such implements, and a large mirror with a frame, also of mirror glass, decorated with stars and other crystal ornaments which I liked a lot.

It was in the morning, about 11 o'clock I think – I can see the bright light of a summer day coming in through the windows, which were open but with the shutters closed.

Mother was brushing her hair, with her maid helping her. I was seated on the ground in the middle of the room, doing something or other – I can't remember what. My nurse Elvira, from Siena, may have been in the room with us – but perhaps not.

Suddenly we heard hurried steps on the narrow internal staircase which connected the dressing room to my father's small private apartment situated on the lower mezzanine just underneath the room where we were. He entered without knocking and said something in an agitated voice. I remember his tone vividly, but not what he said or what the words meant.

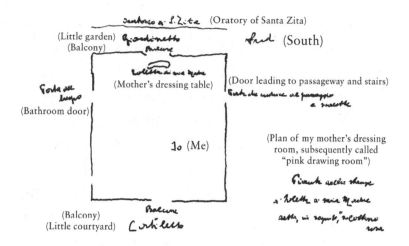

(Oratory of Santa Zita)

(Little garden)
(Balcony)

(South)

(Mother's dressing table)

(Door leading to passageway and stairs)

(Bathroom door)

(Me)

(Plan of my mother's dressing room, subsequently called "pink drawing room")

(Balcony)
(Little courtyard)

Yet I can still "see" quite clearly the effect his words produced: Mother dropped the long-handled silver hairbrush she was holding, while Teresa exclaimed: "*Bon Signour!*"* The whole room was plunged into consternation.

My father* had come to tell us that the previous evening, 29th July 1900, King Umberto had been assassinated at Monza.* I repeat that I can still "see" the stripes of light and shadow coming through the shutters of the balcony window – that I can still "hear" the agitation in my father's voice, the bang of the brush onto the glass surface of the dressing table and Teresa's exclamation in Piedmontese – that I can "feel again" the dismay which filled everyone present. But as far as I'm concerned, all this remains detached from the news of the King's death. Only afterwards was I told about the historical significance of what had happened: it is this which explains why the episode has remained in my memory.

* * *

7

Another memory which I can accurately date is that of the Messina earthquake (28th December 1908).* The shock was felt very clearly in Palermo, but I don't remember it – I think I must have slept through it. However, I can still "see" quite clearly my grandfather's* tall English case clock, then placed incongruously in the large winter drawing room, with its hands stopped at the fatal hour of 5.20 a.m. – and I can still hear one of my uncles (probably Ferdinando, who had a passion for clocks) telling me that it had stopped because of the earthquake on the night before. And I also remember how in the evening of that same day, at about 7.30, while I was in my grandparents' dining room (I often sat with them when they dined, since it was earlier than my own mealtime), one of my uncles – probably Ferdinando again – came in holding a copy of the evening paper with the headline: "Huge Destruction and Many Victims at Messina Following This Morning's Earthquake".

I've said "my grandparents' dining room", but I should really say "my grandmother's",* because my grandfather had already been dead for just over a year.*

This memory is visually much less vivid than the first one, but it is far more precise from the point of view of "what happened".

A few days later, my cousin Filippo, who had lost both his parents in the earthquake, arrived from Messina. He went to live with my Piccolo cousins* – **together with a cousin of his own, Adamo – and I remember going there one bleak,** wintry, rainy day to see him. I remember he (already!) owned a camera, which he had been careful to take with him as he fled the ruins of his home in Via della Rovere, and how he drew the outlines of battleships on a table which stood in front of a window, talking with Casimiro about the calibre of the cannons and the position of the gun towers. His air of detachment, amid the terrible misfortunes that had befallen him, aroused criticism even then among the family, although it was compassionately attributed to the shock (the word used then was "impression") caused by the disaster and common to all the Messina survivors. Afterwards it was put down more correctly to his coldness of character, which was only stirred by technical matters such as, indeed, photography and the position of the gun towers in the early dreadnoughts.*

I remember too my mother's grief when, many days later, the news arrived that the bodies of her sister Lina and her husband had been found. I see Mother seated in the large armchair in the "green drawing room" – a chair no one ever sat in (the same on which, however, I can still see my grandmother sitting) – wearing a short moiré astrakhan cape and sobbing. Large army vehicles were driving through the streets to collect clothing and blankets for the homeless. One of them came down Via Lampedusa, and from one of the balconies I was held out to give two woollen blankets to a soldier who was standing on the vehicle so that he was almost on a level with the balcony. The soldier belonged to the artillery regiment and wore a blue side cap with orange braids – I can still see his ruddy cheeks and hear his accent from Emilia as he thanked me with a "*Grazzie, ragazzo*".* I also remember the remarks people made about the "thoroughly shameless behaviour" of the earthquake survivors, who'd been lodged everywhere in Palermo, including the boxes in theatres, and my father smiling as he said they were keen "to replace the dead" – an allusion I understood all too well.

I have kept no clear memory of my aunt Lina, who died in the earthquake (the first in a series of tragic deaths that befell my mother's sisters, exemplifying the three main ways of coming to a violent end: accident, murder and suicide).* She visited Palermo infrequently – I remember her husband, however, with his lively eyes behind his glasses and a small unkempt beard speckled with grey.

Another day remains impressed on my memory, though I cannot date it precisely: it was certainly long before the earthquake at Messina, perhaps shortly after the death of King Umberto. It was in the middle of the summer, and we were staying with the Florio family at their villa in Favignana.* I remember the nursemaid, Erica, coming and waking me earlier than usual, before 7 o'clock. She sponged my face down quickly in cold water and then dressed me with great care. I was led downstairs and emerged through a small side door into the garden. Then I was made to climb the six or seven steps leading to the front terrace, which looked out onto the sea. I can still recall the blinding sunlight of that morning in July or August. On the terrace, which was sheltered from the sun by large awnings of orange canvas billowing and flapping in the sea breeze like sails (I can still hear the clapping sound they made), my mother, the Signora Florio (the "godlike beauty" Franca)* and others were sitting on wicker chairs. In the middle of them sat a very old lady with a hooked nose, bent with age and dressed in widow's weeds which blew about in the wind. I was brought before her: she said some words I didn't understand and then bent down even further to kiss me on my forehead (I must therefore have been very little if a seated woman needed to bend down to kiss me). After this, I was pulled away and taken back to my room: my Sunday-best clothes were removed and replaced with a plainer outfit, and I was led down to the beach, where I joined the Florio children and others. After bathing in the sea, we spent a long time under the bakingly hot sun playing our favourite game, which consisted in looking in the sand for those tiny pieces of bright-red coral that could often be found in it.

Later in the afternoon, it was revealed to me that the old lady was Eugénie, the former Empress of France.* Her yacht was lying at anchor off the coast of Favignana, and she had been the Florios' guest at dinner the previous evening (something I knew nothing about, of course). In the morning she had come to take her leave (at seven o'clock, imperially indifferent to the torment this caused my mother and the Signora Florio), and the young scions of the families had been duly presented to her. Apparently, the remark she made before kissing me was: *"Quel joli petit!"**

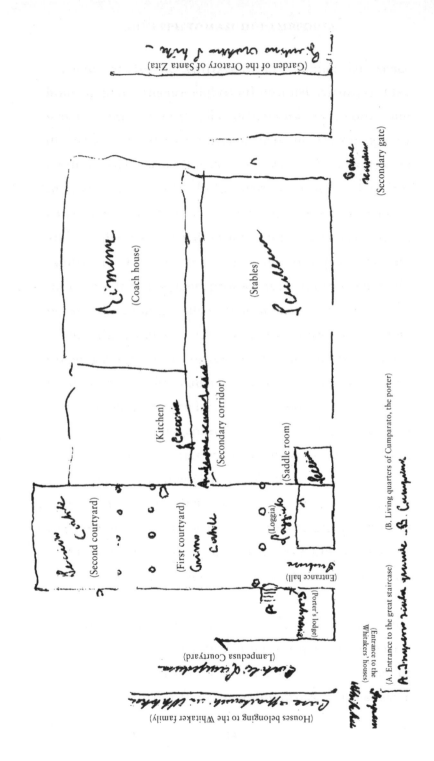

(Garden of the Oratory of Santa Zita)

(Secondary gate)

(Coach house)

(Stables)

(Kitchen)

(Secondary corridor)

(Second courtyard)

(First courtyard)

(Loggia)

(Saddle room)

(Entrance hall)

(Porter's lodge)

(Lampedusa Courtyard)

(Houses belonging to the Whitaker family)

(A. Entrance to the great staircase)

(B. Living quarters of Cumparato, the porter)

(Entrance to the Whitakers' houses)

CHILDHOOD

Places

First of all our house.* I loved it with utter abandon. And I still love it today – now that it has been a mere memory for the past twelve years. Up until a few months before it was destroyed, I slept in the room where I was born, four yards away from where the bed in which my mother had given birth to me had been placed. And I was happy in the certainty that I would die in that same house – perhaps in that very same room. All the other houses I have known – not many, unless you count hotels – have been mere roofs sheltering me from the wind and sun, not HOUSES in the ancient and venerable meaning of the term. **Especially the house I live in now – a house I do not like in the least, which I bought to please my wife and was only too glad to purchase in her name, since it cannot be said truly to be *my* house.**

Therefore it will be a painful task for me to evoke this beloved place that no longer exists in all its completeness and beauty, as it was until 1929 and remained until 5th April 1943, when bombs carried across the Atlantic sought it out and destroyed it.

The first sensation that comes to my mind is its vastness. And this is not because children see their surroundings as larger than they actually are, but because it was so in reality. When I saw the ground it used to stand on covered with its hideous ruins, the area measured over 17,000 square feet. One wing was occupied by us and another by my paternal grandparents, while my unmarried uncles lived on the second floor. I had the run of the entire place for twenty years – its three courtyards, its four terraces, the garden, the huge staircases, its entrance halls and corridors, the stables and service rooms for servants and administrators. For a small boy on his own, it was a veritable kingdom – an empty kingdom which was at times populated with figures full of affection.

I am sure that nowhere on earth was the sky a more intense blue than on that stretch over our enclosed terrace – nor did the sun cast gentler beams of light than it did through the half-closed blinds in the "green drawing room". No curiously shaped patches of damp on the outside walls of courtyards ever excited the imagination more than those found in my house.

I liked everything in that house: the asymmetry of its walls, its numerous drawing rooms, the stucco mouldings of the ceilings, the bad smell in my grandparents' kitchen, the scent of violets in Mother's dressing room, the close warmth of the stables, the pleasant fragrance of clean leather in the saddle room, the mystery of certain half-finished apartments on the second floor, the immense space of our coach house: it was a world full of gentle mysteries, of sweet surprises endlessly renewed.

I was lord of it all and spent my time running about its huge spaces, climbing the grand staircase from the courtyard right up to the loggia on the roof, from which you could see the sea and Monte Pellegrino and the whole city as far as Porta Nuova and Monreale.* And since I knew how to avoid or skirt round all the occupied rooms, I behaved as if I were alone – a lonely dictator with only my beloved Tom often running behind in excited pursuit, his pink tongue hanging out from his sweet black muzzle.

The house – and I insist on calling it a house and not a "palazzo", a term which has since been degraded by being applied to fifteen-storey tower blocks – was concealed in one of the most secluded streets in old Palermo, at No. 17 Via Lampedusa, an ominously unlucky number which merely served to cast a sinister glint on the joys it could offer. (When, later on, the stables were converted to storerooms, we asked for the number to be changed, and it became 23: it was the beginning of the end – the number 17 had brought good fortune to the house).

The street was secluded but not narrow, and it was well paved. Nor was it dirty as one might assume, because opposite the entrance to our house and extending along its entire length there was the ancient Palazzo Pietraperzia, which had no shops or living quarters on the ground floor and displayed an austere but clean façade, painted a decorous white and yellow and punctuated by many windows protected by huge iron grilles, which gave the place the grave but dignified appearance of a convent or state prison. (Later on, the explosion of the bombs dislodged many of these heavy grilles, sending them flying into the rooms of our house opposite: I leave it to the reader to imagine what pleasant effects this might have had on the antique stucco decoration and Murano chandeliers.)

But while Via Lampedusa, or the part of it which ran alongside our house, was decently maintained, the same cannot be said for the streets which led into it. The Via Bara all'Olivella, which connected to Piazza Massimo, heaved with poverty and *catodi*,* and walking along it was a depressing experience. It improved slightly when the Via Roma was opened, but it remained a fairly long stretch of road full of squalor and other horrors.

Architecturally, the façade of our house had nothing distinguished about it: it was painted white, with mustard-yellow for the wide window frames – in other words, it was in the purest seventeenth- or eighteenth-century Sicilian style. The house extended over sixty yards along Via Lampedusa and had nine large balconies looking onto the street. There were two main entrances, almost at the corners of the building, which were, as was usual at the time, enormously wide in order to allow vehicles to turn in even from narrow streets. As a matter of fact, even the four-in-hand my father used to drive so skilfully on race days at Favorita Park could turn in with ease.

The entrance gate was always the one on the left (as you looked at the house from the street), almost at the corner with Via Bara. In the short stretch of wall, just two metres long, between the gate and the side of the building there was the iron-barred window of the porter's lodge. On entering, there was a short passageway paved in stone with white stuccoed walls on either side and a low ledge running along each of these. On the left-hand side was the porter's lodge (with his living quarters behind) and a fine mahogany door with a large pane of frosted glass in the centre, showing the family crest. Immediately after this, still on the left and preceded by two steps, there was the entrance to the "grand staircase" with a double door, again of mahogany and with glass panes inserted – but this time clear glass, without the painted crest. Directly opposite the staircase on the right there was a portico of columns of fine grey Billiemi stone,* which supported the *tocchetto** above. Opposite the gateway was the main courtyard with its cobblestones divided into segments by strips of paving stones. At the end of it were three great arches, on columns again made of Billiemi stone: these supported the terrace that connected the two wings of the house.

There were numerous plants, especially palm trees, ranged under the first colonnade to the right of the passageway in wooden tubs painted green. At the end of the colonnade there was a plaster statue of some Greek god – I couldn't say which one – in a standing pose. There was also the doorway, facing the entrance, to the saddle room.

The "grand staircase" was very beautiful, all made of grey Billiemi stone with two flights of fifteen steps each running between two yellowish walls. Where the second flight of steps began there was a wide, oblong landing with two mahogany doors, one opposite each flight of steps: **the door at the top of the first one led into the mezzanine rooms, which were used for the administrative offices of the house and were known as "Accounting Rooms"; the second door gave onto a tiny closet used by the menservants to change their livery.**

The two doors were framed in Billiemi marble fashioned in the Empire style, while above them, at the level of the first floor, there were two small, gilded bombé balconies, **both giving onto the little entrance lobby of my grandparents' rooms.**

I forgot to say that immediately after the entrance to the staircase – but outside, in the courtyard – was the red bell-pull that the porter had to ring to let the servants know when the family had come back or when visitors had arrived. There was a strict system governing the number of times the bell was rung by the porters, who managed to make – I'm not sure how – the sounds sharp and distinct, without any annoying vibrations: four rings for my grandmother, the Princess, two for her visitors; three for my mother, the

Duchess, and one for her visitors. This system, however, could give rise to misunderstandings: sometimes, when my mother, my grandmother and a friend they had brought back with them returned in the same carriage, a veritable – and endless – concert of 4 + 3 + 2 rings was sounded. The bell was not rung when the men of the family (my grandfather and my father) went out or came back.

At the top of the second flight of stairs was the entrance to the large and well-lit *tocchetto*, a kind of loggia in which the spaces between the columns had been filled, for practical reasons, by large frosted-glass windows with diamond-shaped panes ($\diamondsuit$). There was not much furniture: some large ancestral portraits and, on the left, a big table for incoming mail (I once read a postcard left there addressed to my uncle Ciccio from Paris, with the words of some young French hussy: "*Dis à Moffo qu'il est un mufle*"),* two fine chests and a plaster statue of Pandora in the act of opening the fatal box, surrounded by plants. At the farther end from the top of the staircase was a door which was always kept closed, leading directly into the "green drawing room" (this was the same door which much later became the entrance door to our apartment), while to the right of the staircase – through a door always kept open, covered in quilted red silk and with an upper panel in coloured glass showing the crests of the Lampedusa and Valdina families – was the entrance to the "great hall".

The "great hall" was indeed huge: its floor was tiled with greyish-white marble tiles, and there were three balconies giving onto Via Lampedusa **and one looking out onto the Lampedusa courtyard, a dead-end extension of Via Bara. An arch divided it into two parts – one smaller and one larger.** Much to my parents' chagrin, the decoration of the room was entirely modern, since in 1848 a bomb had fallen on it, destroying its fine painted ceiling and damaging the mural decorations beyond repair. For a long time, or so we were told, a fig tree even flourished in it. The room was restored when my grandfather got married in 1866 or '67, in glossy white stucco with a *lambris** of grey marble. **In the centre of each of the two ceilings the family crest was painted, while opposite the main entrance was a large walnut table where visitors could leave their hats and overcoats, as well as some benches and armchairs.** The servants used to sit here in the "great hall", whiling away the time, ready to jump up and run into the *tocchetto* whenever the above-mentioned bell was rung.

If you went through the previously described red-silk door and turned left, you'd find another door similarly covered in silk, this time green, which led into our apartment. Turning to the left and walking the entire length of the room, you'd reach, on the right, a step and a door leading into my grandparents' apartment, precisely into the small lobby with the two balconies looking onto the grand staircase.

On going through the green-silk door, you'd emerge into an "antechamber" with six ancestral portraits hanging above the balcony and the two doors, grey silk wallpaper, some other paintings and a few pieces of dark-coloured furniture. One's gaze would wander down the row of rooms opening up one after the other along the entire façade. This is where I became fascinated with the magic of light – which in a city like Palermo, where the sunlight is so intense, can vary and change so dramatically even in narrow streets according to the time of day. Sometimes it was softened by the silk curtains in the balcony windows, sometimes it was intensified as it fell on some gilded moulding or was reflected by the yellow damask of an armchair. At times, especially in summer, the rooms were darkened, but you could still sense the powerful light outside filtering through the closed blinds; at other times, depending on the time of day, a single ray penetrated into the room, straight and sharply outlined as if from Mount Sinai,* with myriads of dust motes swarming as it fell on the rugs and gave their hue – invariably a ruby-red in each room – a new vividness. My soul could never break free from that enthralling spell of light and colour. Every now and then, in some old palace or church, I come across that same quality of light – and my soul would melt away if I didn't at once fire off some wicked joke.*

After the anteroom came the one known as the "*lambris*" room, since the lower half of its walls were decorated with carved-walnut *lambris*. This was followed by the "supper room", where the walls were covered by orange-coloured hangings with a floral pattern: bits of them still survive in my wife's room's upholstery. Then there was the ball-room, with its floor of enamelled tiles and its ceilings on which a delicious tangle of gold and yellow tracery framed mythological scenes crowded with all the gods of Olympus, rustically sturdy amid great billows of drapery. After this room came my mother's boudoir, which was very beautiful, with its antique ceiling covered with flowers and branches in painted stucco, in a design that had all the shapeliness and tenderness of one of Mozart's melodies.

From there you entered into Mother's bedroom, which was very spacious: its largest part made up the corner of the house, with a balcony (the last one along the façade) looking out onto Via Lampedusa and another one overlooking the garden of the Oratory of Santa Zita. The decorations – in wood, stucco and fresco – were among the most beautiful in the entire house.

Turning left from the "*lambris*" room, you would enter the "green drawing room", which opened onto the "yellow drawing room" and, farther down, into a room that was at first used as my day nursery,* then transformed into the "red drawing room" (where most of our time was spent) and later into the library. As you entered from the yellow drawing room, you'd see on your left a window giving onto the main courtyard and a glass door leading onto the terrace. At a right angle to these was a door (which was afterwards walled up) to a small room that had been my grandfather's bathroom (complete with marble tub) and was later used to store my toys, and another glass door leading onto a small terrace.

Childhood – Places – Other Houses

The beauty of our "house" in Palermo was complemented by other properties in the country. There were four of them: Santa Margherita di Belice, the villa at Bagheria, the palazzo in Torretta and the country house in Raitano. There was also the house at Palma and the Castle of Montechiaro, but we never visited those.*

These Houses and Their Destinies

Our favourite house was the one at Santa Margherita, where we spent months at a time, even in winter. It was one of the most beautiful country houses I have ever seen. Dating from 1680, it had been completely rebuilt by Prince Cutò around 1810, when Ferdinand IV and Maria Carolina were forced to reside in Sicily for a very long time as Murat ruled over Naples.* After their stay, however, it had not been abandoned like all the other houses in Sicily, but kept in good condition, restored and improved up to the time of my grandmother Cutò.* She had been brought up in France until the age of twenty, and was therefore free of the usual Sicilian distaste for country life. She lived at Santa Margherita most of the time and had brought the house up to date* in terms of comfort* (that is to say, according to the standards of the Second Empire, which were not so different from those maintained until 1914).

The Journey

I began to experience that vague, not totally graspable thrill of adventure which forms such a large part of my memories of Santa Margherita during our journey there. That was an undertaking full of inconvenience and appeal. There were no cars in those days: in around 1905 the only vehicle to be seen in the streets of Palermo was the *électrique** belonging to the elderly Giovanna Florio. From Lolli station there was a train leaving at 5.10 a.m., so we needed to get up at half-past three in order to catch it. That was always a disagreeable hour to be woken up – but I loathed it even more, since whenever I had a tummy ache it was the time of night I'd be given a good old dose of castor oil. The household servants and cooks had already left the day before. We all climbed into two closed landaus: in the first were Mother and Father, myself and, say, my governess Anna I.* In the second were Mother's maid – either Teresa or Concettina – our accountant Ferrara,* who hailed from Santa Margherita and would be spending his holidays with his family, and Paolo, my father's valet. I think there was also a third vehicle carrying the luggage and the lunch baskets.

We usually left at the end of June: dawn would just be breaking over the deserted streets. Crossing Piazza Politeama and going down Via Dante (which was then called Via Esposizione), we would arrive at Lolli station. There we all tumbled into the train for Trapani. At that time train carriages had no corridors, and therefore no toilets: when I was a very little boy, an ugly brown ceramic chamberpot, bought especially for the journey, would be brought along for me and thrown out of the window before the train reached its destination. The ticket collector did his rounds gripping onto the outside of the train: at a certain point his braided cap and black-gloved hand would suddenly appear in the window.

For hours on end we travelled across the beautiful and profoundly melancholy landscape of western Sicily – Carini, Cinisi, Lo Zucco, Partinico – which I am sure at that time was still exactly as Garibaldi's Thousand had found it when they landed.* Then the train ran along the coast, and the railway seemed to rest on the sand; the sun, already high in the sky, baked us in our iron box. There were no thermos flasks back then, and none of the stations offered refreshments. The train then turned inland, winding between stony mountains and harvested wheat fields, tawny as a lion's coat. Finally, at 11 we arrived at Castelvetrano,* which back then was not the spruce and up-and-coming town of today but a lugubrious village with open sewers, pigs strutting down the main street and billions of flies. Our carriages, two

landaus fitted with yellow awnings, were waiting for us at
the station, which had already been roasting under the hot
sun for six hours.

At half-past eleven we would set off again. For about an
hour, as far as Partanna,* the road was easy and wound
level through a beautiful landscape of cultivated fields. As
we rode on, we'd recognize places, the two majolica Negro
heads on the pilasters at the gates of a villa, or the iron
cross marking the spot where someone had been murdered.
When we reached Partanna, however, there was a change of
scene: three Carabinieri – a *brigadiere** and two soldiers – on
horseback and with white handkerchiefs protecting the back
of their necks from the sun like Fattori's light cavalrymen*
were assigned to escort us to Santa Margherita. The road
then started to climb: all around us stretched the endless
and empty landscape of feudal Sicily, without a breath of
air, stark under the blazing sun. We'd look out for a tree
under whose branches we could stop and have our lunch,
but there were only thin olive trees offering no shade. Finally
we'd come across an abandoned farmhouse, half in ruins
but with all its windows carefully closed: we'd get down
from the carriages to eat in its shade – the food was usually
tasty. Sitting slightly apart from us, the Carabinieri, who
were in a merry mood and already sunburnt, lunched on
the bread and meat and pudding and bottles of wine we'd
sent over to them. At the end of the meal, the *brigadiere*
came over holding a full glass in his hand: "Also on behalf

of my officers, I'd like to thank your Excellencies" – and he knocked back the wine, which by then must have heated up to over 40 degrees.

One of the soldiers, however, remained standing and patrolled round the house, keeping a lookout.

We climbed back into the carriages. It was two o'clock: the very worst time of day in summer in rural Sicily. The horses ambled down the road as we descended towards the Belice river. A silence settled over us – above the sound of the horses' hooves could only be heard the voice of a Carabiniere humming: "A Spanish woman knows how to love."* A cloud of dust enveloped us. [**Anna I, who had also been in India…**]

We then crossed the Belice – which passed for a proper river in Sicily, even with only a trickle of water in its bed – and started the interminable climb at an ambling pace, with never-ending twists and turns along the road through the parched landscape.

It seemed as though it would never end – and yet it did end: at the top of the slope the horses stopped, shaking and sweating, the Carabinieri climbed down from their saddles and we too got off to stretch our legs. Then we set off again at a rapid trot. Mother began to alert me: "Keep a lookout now: on the left you'll soon see the Venaria." And it was true: we went over a bridge, and there, on the left, you could see at last some clumps of green trees, reed groves and even an orange orchard. This was Dagali, the first property on the

Cutò estate you came across on the journey. Behind Dagali there was a steep hill with a wide road, lined with cypress trees, winding up all the way to the Venaria, the hunting lodge which belonged to us.*

We were nearly there. Mother was so in love with the place that she could no longer sit still: she'd lean out to look now on one side, now on the other. "We're almost at Montevago. We're home!" And we were indeed driving through Montevago, the first sign of life we had seen for four hours – if sign of life is the right expression! Wide empty streets, poverty-stricken houses under the unrelenting sun – not a human creature to be seen, just a few pigs and some scrawny cats.

But once we had left Montevago behind, everything started to improve. The road ran straight and level through pleasant countryside. "Look, there's Giambalvo's villa! And there's the Church of Our Lady of Grace and its cypresses!" Even the sight of the cemetery was greeted with joy. Then came the Church of Our Lady of Trapani. We'd arrived! Here was the bridge…

It was 5 o'clock in the afternoon. We'd been travelling for 12 hours.

Standing on the bridge was the municipal band, who launched with zest into a polka. Worn out as we were from the journey, our faces white with dust and our throats burning with thirst, we made an effort to smile and to thank them. Then, after going down a few streets, we came out into the main square, saw the elegant façade of the house and entered through the gateway – into the first courtyard, through the passageway, into the second courtyard. We'd arrived. At the foot of the external staircase there was a small delegation of the household staff, led by the worthy Don Nofrio,* with his white beard, tiny next to his imposing wife.

"Welcome!"

"We're so happy to be here!"

Upstairs, in one of the drawing rooms, Don Nofrio had glasses of iced lemonade ready for us – the lemonade was bad, yet it was blissful to drink. Anna then dragged me upstairs to my room, where, reluctantly, I got into a bath of lukewarm water, which the ever-attentive Don Nofrio had had prepared for me, while my poor parents had to deal with the stream of acquaintances who had started to arrive.

The House*

It was right in the middle of the town, in the tree-shaded main square, and was of immense size, comprising all together three hundred rooms, small and large. Just to give you an idea, it resembled a kind of Vatican, a closed and autonomous complex: there were public reception rooms, private sitting rooms, guest quarters that could accommodate up to thirty people, living quarters for domestic staff, three huge courtyards, stables and coach houses, a private theatre and a church, a vast and extremely beautiful garden and a large orchard.

And what rooms! Prince Niccolò had been almost unique among his peers in having had the good taste to leave the eighteenth-century rooms unchanged. In the great apartment each door was framed on either side by inventively designed eighteenth-century marble friezes in grey, black or red, which with their harmonious asymmetry sounded a kind of jubilant fanfare as you passed from one room to the next. In the second courtyard a broad staircase with a green marble balustrade led, with a single flight of steps, up to a terrace where there was the main entrance gate, surmounted by a cross adorned with nine bells.*

From the terrace you entered into a colossal anteroom, whose walls were covered by two rows, one above the other, of full-length life-size portraits of Filangeri ancestors from 1080 to my grandmother's father, dressed in a huge variety of costumes, from a crusader's to that of Ferdinand II's gentleman of the royal bedchamber.* Despite their very mediocre painterly qualities, they gave the immense room an atmosphere of liveliness and familiarity. Beneath each portrait there was a label – black with white lettering – with the names and titles of the persons portrayed, together with the significant events of their life: "Riccardo, who defended Antioch against the infidel" – "Raimondo, who died in the defence of Acri" – another Riccardo, "the leading instigator of the Sicilian rebellion" (in other words, the Sicilian Vespers) – Niccolò I, "who commanded two Hussar regiments against the Gallic hordes in 1796".*

Also, above every door or window, there were panoramic maps of the various fiefs – almost all of them still belonging to the family at that time. In the four corners of the room there were – in obeyance to the taste of the time – four bronze statues of warriors in armour holding aloft simple oil lamps. Up on the ceiling, Jove, wrapped in a purple cloud, bestowed his blessing on Angerius* as he embarked on the voyage from his native Normandy for Sicily, with a throng of tritons and sea nymphs surrounding the galleys which were about to set sail on the mother-of-pearl sea. [**Campieri – caps, uniforms, rifles, hares...**]

But once you had got beyond this prelude, so to speak, full of ancestral family pride, the house became entirely graceful and ingratiating – or, rather, veiled its pride with an outward amiability just as an aristocrat conceals his under habitual courtesy. There was the library housed in cabinets designed in that delightful eighteenth-century Sicilian style known as *stile di badia*,* similar to the elaborate Venetian manner, but more robust and less mawkish. Almost all the works of the Enlightenment philosophers were there, in tawny, gilded bindings: the *Encyclopédie*, Voltaire, Fontenelle, Helvétius, the great Kehl edition of Voltaire (if Maria Carolina read this, what can she have thought of it?); then there was *Victoires et conquêtes*, a collection of Napoleonic news-sheets and war reports which I used to love reading in the long silent afternoons stretched out face down on one of the vast *poufs* which occupied the centre of the ballroom. It was in short a bizarre library to have been put together by a reactionary like Prince Niccolò. There were also bound collections of satirical journals from the Risorgimento period, such as the *Fischietto* and the *Spirito folletto*, several fine editions of *Don Quixote* and of La Fontaine, the *History of Napoleon* by Norvins with its splendid illustrations (I still have that book), pretty much the complete works of Zola, whose bright-yellow covers stood out impertinently in that mellow room, and a few mediocre novels, but also a copy of *I Malavoglia*, with an autograph dedication from the author.*

I do not know whether in what I have written so far I have been able to convey the idea that I was a boy who enjoyed solitude, who liked the company of objects rather than people. Since this was the case, it is easy to understand how ideally suited to me the life at Santa Margherita was. In the ornate vastness of the house (**12 people in 300 rooms**) I wandered about as in an enchanted forest with no hidden dragons but full of pleasant marvels – even in the delightful names of the rooms: the "room of little birds", with its walls covered in hangings of raw silk, rough to the touch, where amid an endless tangle of flowering branches little hand-painted birds gleamed in their many-coloured plumages; or the "monkeys' room", where hairy, mischievous *ouistitis** dangled from tropical trees; or "Ferdinando's rooms", a name which for me before anything else conjured up an image of my fair-haired grinning uncle, but instead derived from this having been the private apartment of the jolly and cruel "King Big Nose" himself* – as indeed the presence of a huge Empire-style *lit-bateau* also testified, with its mattress wrapped in a kind of morocco-leather casing, which appears to have been used instead of blankets for royal beds. The morocco was green and thickly engraved with the Bourbon emblem of three gilded lilies: it had the appearance of an enormous book. The walls were covered in lighter-green silk, with alternating vertical stripes of glossy and hatched matt cloth, identical to that found in the "green drawing room" in our Palermo house. The "tapestry room" was the only room to which a sinister association later attached itself. There were eight large *succhi d'erba** depicting episodes from the *Gerusalemme Liberata.** One of them showed the duel between Tancredi and Argante – and one of their horses had a strangely human gaze, a feature which I later connected with Poe's 'House of the Metzengerstein'.* This particular *succo d'erba* still belongs to me.*

Curiously we always spent the evenings in the ballroom, which was the central room on the first floor, with eight balconies looking onto the piazza and four more with a view onto the first courtyard. It was similar to the ballroom in the house in Palermo. Gold was the dominant motif in this room. The wallpaper was a soft, pale shade of green, but this was almost completely covered with hand-embroidered golden flowers and foliage, while the wooden skirting board and the enormous shutters as tall as a gateway were painted in a pure matt gold with lustrous gold decorations. When, on winter evenings (and we spent two whole winters at Santa Margherita, as my mother never really wanted to leave), we sat round the central hearth in the feeble glow cast by a few oil lamps, the light from the fire would flicker whimsically over flowers on the wallpaper and mouldings on the shutters, and it was as if we were shut inside a fairy's jewel box. I can date one of these evenings precisely, since I remember the newspapers being brought in with reports of the fall of Port Arthur.*

These evenings were not restricted to the family circle – indeed, they almost never were. My mother was inclined to continue the tradition begun by her parents of maintaining cordial relations with the local dignitaries: many of them were invited by turns to dine with us, and twice a week all of them gathered to play *scopone** in that very ballroom. My mother had known them all since she was little and was fond of them; to me they seemed – although perhaps in reality they were not – without exception excellent people. There was Don Peppino Lomonaco from Palermo, whose severely reduced financial circumstances had forced him to move to Santa Margherita, where he owned a tiny house and an even smaller holding of land. An enthusiastic hunter, he had been a close friend of my grandfather and enjoyed particularly good treatment: I think he had lunch with us every day and was the only person who addressed my mother with the informal "*tu*", whereas she always used a respectful "*Lei*" to him in return. He was a little old man, lean and straight, with blue eyes and a long white drooping moustache, of a distinguished and even elegant appearance in his frayed but well-cut suits. I now suspect he may have been an illegitimate offspring of the Cutò family – in short, my mother's uncle. He played the piano and used to tell us about the amazing hunting feats that took place while he was out with Grandfather through the thickets and underbrush, as well as the extraordinarily sharp senses of his two bitch hounds (Diana and Furetta) and the anxious but always in the end harmless encounters with the gangs of the brigands Leone and Capraro. Then there was Nenè Giaccone, one of the leading local landowners, with his fiery-red goatee and unquenchable vivacity: he was regarded by the locals as a great *bon viveur*, since every year he spent two months in Palermo, at the Hotel Milano in Via Emerico Amari, next to the Politeama, which was considered *fast*.*

There was the Cavaliere Mario Rossi, short with a small black beard, a former official in the postal services who was always talking about Frascati ("You see, Your Grace, Frascati is *almost* Rome"), where he had once spent a few months of his career. There was Ciccio Neve, with his large ruddy cheeks and side whiskers *à la* Franz Joseph,* who lived with a mad sister (if you get to know a Sicilian village well, you'll find innumerable mad people in it); Catania, the local schoolmaster, with a Moses-like beard; Montalbano, another large local landowner and the epitome of what is meant by a "village baron" – obtuse and gross, the father, I believe, of the present Communist member of parliament; Giorgio di Giuseppe, who was the intellectual of the group and who could be heard, when you passed under his windows in the evening, playing Chopin nocturnes on the piano; Giambalvo, hugely fat and very witty; Dottor Monteleone, with his black goatee, who had studied in Paris and often spoke of the "Rue Monge" and the extraordinary adventures he had had there; Don Colicchio Terrasa, extremely aged and practically a peasant, together with his famously gluttonous son, Totò; and many others, who were seen less frequently.

It will have been noted that the group consisted only of men: their wives, daughters and sisters stayed at home, either because it was not the custom for women in the town to pay calls (in the period from 1905 to 1914) or because their husbands, fathers and brothers did not consider them to be presentable. My mother and father visited each of them once during every annual stay in Santa Margherita; on occasion they were also the luncheon guests of Mario Rossi, whose wife came from the Billela family and was celebrated for her culinary skills. Sometimes, using a complicated system of advance notices and other preliminary warnings, she would send over to us, by means of a young lad who would sprint across the square under the blazing sun, an immense tureen filled with *maccheroni di zito alla siciliana* – a sauce of minced meat, aubergines and basil – which I remember as a dish worthy of being set before the primeval country gods. The boy who carried it over had precise instructions to put the bowl down on the dining table when we were already seated – and before taking his leave he would enjoin: "*'A Signura raccumanna: 'u cascavaddu.*"* Sensible advice no doubt, but we never followed it.

There was one exception to the absence of women: Margherita, the daughter of Nenè Giaccone the *bon viveur*, who had been educated at the Sacro Cuore school. She was an attractive young girl with flame-coloured hair like her father's, and every now and then she would turn up.

In contrast to the cordial relations which existed with the people of the town, those with the local authorities were strained: the Mayor, Don Pietro Giaccone, never called on us – nor did the parish priest, even though the Cutò family owned the benefice. The endless quarrels with the council over the "local by-laws" account for the absence of the Mayor. Giaccone was quite the gallant man, and for a while he lived with a young hussy who passed herself off as Spanish, called Pepita. He had picked her up in a *café chantant* in Agrigento (!). She drove round the streets of the town in a *charrette* drawn by a grey pony. One day my father was standing in front of the main entrance and saw this elegant vehicle pass by with the couple in it. He saw – he had an infallible eye for such things – that the fork had slipped out of the hub and the wheel was about to fall off – so, although he had never met the honourable personage in question and relations were already strained, he ran after the *charrette* shouting: "Cavaliere, watch out, the right wheel is going to fall off!"

The Cavaliere stopped the cart, raised his horsewhip in salutation, and said: "Thanks, I'll see to it" – and the cart started off again without his getting down. After twenty yards the wheel did indeed come to a sorry end, and the honourable gentleman together with Pepita in her pink chiffon gown were rudely tumbled out onto the road. They didn't hurt themselves much. On the following day, four partridges and a visiting card appeared: "From Cavaliere Pietro Giaccone, Mayor of Santa Margherita Belice, with thanks for the good advice which he chose to ignore."

But this sign of an improvement in relations never led to anything.

The last and the largest of the three courtyards of the house at Santa Margherita was known as the "courtyard of the palm trees", since a circle of very tall palm trees heavy with bunches of unpollinated dates was planted round it. Entering through the passageway which connected from the second courtyard, you had on the right the long low line of the block of stables and, beyond, the riding ground. In the centre of the courtyard, leaving the stables and the riding ground to your right, there were two tall pillars in porous yellow stone, decorated with large masks and festoons, through which steps led down to the garden. The flights of steps were all short (less than a dozen steps), but within this limited space the Baroque architect had succeeded in giving vent to a devilish inventiveness: high and low steps alternated, and the short flights took sudden unexpected twists and turns, thus creating superfluous landings with niches and benches on them. In this way, within such a contracted depth, a whole system of possible motions was created, of coming together and moving apart, of brusque repudiations and affectionate encounters, which gave the sequence of steps the feel of a lovers' quarrel.

The garden, like so many others in Sicily, had been created on a plot of ground on a lower level than the house, in order to take advantage – or so I believe – of a spring gushing out there. It was very large and, seen from one of the windows in the house, its complicated pattern of avenues and pathways seemed perfectly regular. It was full of holm oaks and monkey-puzzle trees, and the avenues were bordered with hedges of box myrtle. In the intense heat of summer, when the spring was reduced to a trickle, it was a paradise of scorched, dry fragrances, of wild marjoram and calamint – like so many Sicilian gardens, which often seem to exist more for the pleasures of smell than of sight.

The broad avenue which ran round the four sides of the garden was the only straight pathway there. For the rest, the designer (who, to judge from his bizarre inventiveness, must have been the same architect responsible for the stairs) had created endless twists and turns, passages and mazes, so that the garden had the same air of gentle mystery which enveloped the whole house. All these criss-crossing paths however ended up in a great open space at the centre of the garden, in the place where the spring had first been discovered: now enclosed in an ornate prison, it sent merry jets into the huge fountain: right in the middle of it, on an island of artificial ruins, the long-haired and loose-robed Goddess of Plenty poured torrents of water into the deep basin of the fountain, rippled with friendly waves. It was enclosed by a balustrade on which statues of tritons and nereids had been placed at intervals, in the pose of getting ready to dive: seen individually, their gestures seemed unco-ordinated, but when they were looked at all together they formed a scenic whole. Dotted all around the central space with the fountain were stone benches, coated and darkened with ancient mildew, **and protected from the wind and sun by the dense foliage of the trees overhead.**

But for a child the garden was brimful of surprises. In one corner there was a large greenhouse filled with cactus plants and rare shrubs: this was the realm of Nino the head gardener, a great friend of mine. He too was red-haired, like so many other locals, perhaps as a consequence of the Norman Filangeris. There was a bamboo grove which grew thickly and sturdily round a secondary fountain, and in its shade a playground with a swing – the same one from which, long before my time, Pietro Scalea,* later to become the minister for war, had fallen and broken his arm. Built into the wall along one of the side avenues, there was a huge cage once intended for monkeys. One Sunday morning, when the garden was open for local people to visit, my cousin Clementina Trigona and I shut ourselves in it, leaving the astonished visitors to gape, speechless and perplexed, at these dressed-up apes.

Then there was the "dolls' house", in red brick with windows framed with *pietra serena*, which had been built for my mother and her four sisters to play in. Now with its roof fallen through and its floors collapsed, it was the only part of this large garden which left one feeling disconsolate – Nino kept the rest in admirable order, with every tree well pruned, all the pathways bright with yellow sand and their hedges properly trimmed.

Every fortnight a cart climbed up from the nearby Belice river carrying a huge barrel of eels, which were released into the secondary fountain (the one in the bamboo grove); this was used as a fishpond, and the cook, whenever it was required in the kitchen, would send someone down with a net to fish out the eels.

In every corner of the avenues there were busts of obscure ancient gods, normally without their noses – and, as should be the case in any self-respecting Eden, there was a serpent lurking in the shade, in the form of several bushes of castor-oil plants (which were actually very beautiful, with their oval green leaves bordered with red): one day these gave me a nasty surprise when I crushed a pretty little bunch of crimson berries and breathed in the smell of that oil, which in that happy time was the only real shadow darkening my existence. I gave my oily hand to my beloved dog Tom (who had followed me) to sniff, and I can still see the movement, polite but full of reproach, with which he slightly lifted his upper lip, as well-brought up dogs do when they want to show their disgust without offending their masters.

The garden, as I've said, was full of surprises – but then so was the entire house at Santa Margherita: it was full of the most enchanting little traps. You would open a door in a corridor and glimpse a long succession of rooms plunged in the shade of the half-closed shutters and walls covered in French prints depicting Bonaparte's Italian campaigns. At the top of the stairs to the second floor there was a door which was almost invisible as it was so narrow and flush with the wall: it opened into a large room with its walls hung from top to bottom with old paintings, like those you see in engravings of the eighteenth-century *Salon** in Paris. One of the ancestral portraits in the anteroom was movable and, right behind, were the rooms in which my grandfather, that mighty hunter before the Lord,* kept his hunting paraphernalia. The trophies displayed in glass cases were all local: partridges **with their red talons**, wistful-looking woodcocks, coots from the Belice valley. But the bench with its scales and presses and measuring implements used to prepare the cartridges – the cupboards with their glass doors full of multicoloured cartridge cases and the coloured prints showing more extreme adventures (I can still see a bearded explorer dressed in white screaming as he flees from a greenish rhinoceros charging at him) – these things captivated an adolescent boy. There were also, hanging on the walls, prints and photographs of hounds, pointers and setters, emanating the calm tenderness so typical of dogs' facial expressions. Large racks held the rifles, each labelled with a number which corresponded to a register where the shots fired from each weapon were listed. It was from one of these rifles – a woman's model, I think, with a richly damascened double barrel – that I fired, in the garden, the first and the last shots of my cynegetic career.* One of the bearded *campieri** forced me to shoot at some innocent robins. Unhappily, two fell, with blood sprinkled on their warm fluffy grey feathers. As they were still breathing, the *campiere* crushed their heads between his fingers.

For all my reading of *Victoires et conquêtes* with phrases like "*l'épée de l'intrépide général comte Delort rougie du sang des ennemis de l'Empire*",* the scene horrified me: it was clear I only enjoyed the idea of blood when it was transformed into a metaphor by printers' ink. I went straight to my father – it was he who had wanted this Massacre of the Innocents – and declared that I would never shoot another living thing.

Ten years later I had to kill a Bosnian with a pistol shot and God knows how many other people with cannon fire, but it made a much smaller impression on me than the poor robins had done.

There was also the "carriage room" – a huge dark space housing two immense eighteenth-century *carrosses*. One was a ceremonial coach, all gilded, with glass windows and doors painted with pastoral scenes in *vernis Martin** against a yellow background. Inside, there were seats upholstered in faded yellow taffeta for at least six people. The other carriage was for travel – olive green with gilded edgings and, on the doors, **lined with green morocco leather,** the family crest. Underneath the seats there were padded receptacles in which, I assume, provisions for the journey could be stored. A solitary silver plate was all that remained.

Then there was the "girls' kitchen", with its miniature fireplace and range of copper pans on the same scale, which my grandmother had had installed in the vain hope it would entice her daughters to learn how to cook.

And there was the church and the theatre, which one reached through a series of marvellous passageways – but I will speak about these later.

In contrast with such splendours, the room where I slept was totally bare. It looked onto the garden and was called "the pink room", because it was *painted* in gleaming stucco, **the exact hue of a pink Maréchal Niel rose.** On one side there was the dressing room, with a curious oval copper bathtub standing on four high wooden legs. I remember that sometimes, when I was made to have a bath, starch was dissolved in the bathwater, or a bag of bran that created a fragrant milky drizzle once soaked.

These were *bains de son** – a custom you find mentioned in memoirs dating from the period of the Second Empire and that my grandmother must have handed down to my mother.

An adjoining room which was identical to mine, except for being painted blue, was where the various governesses I had in turn slept: Anna I, followed by Anna II, both German, and then Mademoiselle, who was French. Above my bedhead there was a Louis XVI display cabinet in white wood with three small ivory statues of the Holy Family against a crimson background. By some miracle this cabinet survives and now hangs above the bed in which I sleep in the villa belonging to my Piccolo cousins at Capo d'Orlando.* But it is not only the statuettes of the Holy Family I find again in the villa: I rediscover a vestige – a frail one, to be sure, but quite definite – of my childhood at Santa Margherita, and this is the reason I like going there so much.

There was also the church, which was also the town's main church. Coming out of the carriage room and turning left, you climbed a staircase leading to a wide corridor, at the end of which was the "study room", a kind of classroom with benches, blackboards and relief maps, where my mother and aunts had studied as little girls.

Before reaching this room, there were two doors on the left which led into three guest rooms. These were the most sought after in the house, since they looked onto the terrace at the top of the great entrance stairway. On the right,

instead, between two white console tables, there was a large yellow door giving access to a small oblong room, with chairs and various shelves filled with devotional images. I remember a large ceramic plate with a life-size head of John the Baptist standing in the middle and the coagulated blood at the back. From this room one entered the gallery, positioned at the level of a high first floor and surrounded by a beautiful wrought-iron balustrade gilded with floral decoration and looking directly onto the high altar. There were prie-dieus and seats and innumerable rosaries: it was in the gallery that we attended Mass every Sunday at eleven – a Mass sung without excessive fervour. The church itself, I recall, was spacious and beautiful, built in Empire style with some large ugly frescoes set between the white stucco decorations on the ceiling, like the ones in the Olivella church in Palermo,* of which the one in Santa Margherita was an imitation on a smaller scale.

Again from the "carriage room" – I now realize this was a kind of *plaque tournante** – you could reach all the less frequented parts of the house: if you went to the right, you were led into a series of passageways, cubbyholes and short flights of steps from which, as in certain dreams, you had the vague impression you would never find the way out, but which finally came out in the corridor of the theatre. This was a proper theatre, with two tiers of 12 boxes each, together with a gallery and, naturally, the stalls. It could seat at least three hundred. The auditorium was all white and gold, with the benches and walls in the boxes upholstered in much-faded blue velvet. The style was Louis XVI, unshowy and elegant. At the centre was the equivalent of a royal box, reserved for our family and surmounted by an enormous gilt-wood trophy: a double-headed eagle with a bell-adorned cross on its breast.* The painted drop curtain, of a later date, depicted Riccardo Filangeri engaged in the defence of Antioch* (if Grousset* is to be believed, the defence was a lot less heroic than the painter's depiction of thc story).

The auditorium was lit by gilded oil lamps on projecting brackets under the first tier of boxes.

The wonderful thing about this theatre (which also had an entrance in the square for the general public) was that it was often in use.

Every now and then a troupe of strolling comic actors – or *guitti* – would arrive, usually in summer, when they moved on carts from one village to another, performing in each for two or three days. In Santa Margherita, where there was a proper theatre, they stayed longer, for a fortnight or so.

At 10 in the morning the chief of the troupe, in frock coat and top hat, would come to ask permission to hold performances in the theatre. He was received by my father or, in his absence, by my mother, who naturally gave their permission, refused any rent (or rather drew up a contract in which a nominal sum of 50 centesimi was paid for the fortnight) and even paid the subscription for our "box". After that, the chief of the troupe left, only to return half an hour later to ask if we could lend some pieces of furniture. Indeed these troupes travelled with only a few pieces of painted scenery and without any furniture, which would have been too costly and cumbersome to transport. The furniture was handed over, and in the evening we would recognize our armchairs, tables and hat stands on the stage (I am sorry to say we never gave them the best pieces). They were duly returned to us when the time came for them to leave: sometimes they had been given a new lick of paint, but it was done so badly that other troupes had to be asked to desist from this well-meaning practice. **As I remember,** on one occasion the leading actress also came to see us, a stout woman from Ferrara, about thirty years old, who was to play the "Lady of the Camellias"* in the closing night of the season. She could find nothing to wear in her own wardrobe that would be appropriate for the solemnity of the occasion and asked my mother to lend her some evening dresses. And so the "Lady of the Camellias" appeared that evening in a very low-cut *vert Nil** dress covered in silver sequins.

There are no longer any troupes of actors travelling from village to village in the countryside – and it is a great shame. The staging was barely adequate, and clearly the actors were bad, but they took their roles seriously and acted with enthusiasm – and their "presence" on stage was a good deal more real than the pale shadows in the third-rate films that get shown today in these same villages.

There was a performance each evening, and the repertoire was vast, drawn from the whole of nineteenth-century drama: Scribe, Rovetta, Sardou, Giacometti and also Torelli.* There was once a performance of *Hamlet*: that was the first time I saw it. The audience, made up in part of local peasants, listened attentively and applauded with enthusiasm. In Santa Margherita, at least, these troupes enjoyed excellent business, what with the theatre being rent-free and the furniture likewise, and the horses which pulled their carts lodged and fed in our own stables.

I would go every evening, except for the one performance in the season known as the "black evening", when some supposedly indecent French *pochade** would be performed. On the following day our friends in the town would come to report on the licentious show, and were usually very disappointed that it had turned out to be less indecent than they thought.

I enjoyed myself a lot, and so did my parents. For the best troupes, at the end of their season, we held a sort of garden party* with a rustically plain but plentiful buffet, so that those excellent *guitti* could fill their stomachs – which too often I fear might have gone empty.

By 1921, the last year I spent a long time in Santa Margherita, troupes of actors no longer came, and instead flickering films were being shown. The war had killed off, among other things, these troupes of strolling actors, which in all their picturesque poverty served an artistic purpose:

I believe they were the breeding ground of many of Italy's greatest actors, including Duse.*

But I've just realized I've forgotten to describe the dining room at Santa Margherita, which was peculiar for many reasons – above all, for the fact that there *was* one. I believe it's very rare in any eighteenth-century house to find a room expressly designed for dining in: in that period meals were taken in any room, and the room where one dined changed all the time, as indeed is my habit today.

But in the house at Santa Margherita a dining room existed: it wasn't very large, and could comfortably seat only about twenty diners. It had two balconies looking onto the second courtyard, **and three doors. The main one led into the "picture gallery" (different from the one I've already described), another communicated with the "hunting rooms", while a third opened into the "office",* where there was a small lift operated by a rope pulley down to the kitchen below.** These doors were white, in Louis XVI style, with large panels decorated in relief with gilded mouldings in a lustreless greenish gold. A lantern-shaped Murano lamp hung from the ceiling: on the greyish background of its glass stood out delicately coloured flowers.

Prince Alessandro* had been responsible for the room's furnishings, and it had been his idea to decorate the walls with depictions of himself together with his family as they had their meals. These pictures on canvas were huge, completely covering each wall, from floor to ceiling, with almost life-sized figures. One showed breakfast: the Prince, wearing a green hunting dress, in his boots and holding a hat, and the Princess, in a white *déshabillé* but wearing jewels, were seated at a small table drinking chocolate, waited on by a small black slave wearing a turban. She was holding out a biscuit to an impatient hound, while he lifted a large blue cup decorated with a floral design to his lips. Another painting showed a picnic: numerous ladies and gentlemen were seated round a tablecloth spread out on the grass, on which magnificent pies and wine bottles cased in straw had been placed. In the background a fountain could be seen, with short saplings – it must have been the garden at Santa Margherita just after it was first laid out and planted.

A third painting – also the largest – showed a grand formal banquet, with all the men in curly white wigs and the ladies in their finery. The Princess wore an enchanting pink silk gown with silver brocade, a *collier de chien** round her neck and a large ruby necklace over her chest. The waiters were in ceremonial livery and family chains, and were carrying into the room fabulously inventive dishes piled high in salvers.

There were two more of these paintings, but I only remember one of them, because it was always in front of me. It showed children at their teatime: two little girls, about 10-12 years old, sitting up straight in tight, pointed bodices with their faces powdered, were opposite a boy of about fifteen, wearing an orange jacket with black cuffs and sporting a dress sword, and an elderly lady dressed in black (no doubt their governess). They were eating tall, sharp-pointed ice creams of a strange pink colour, possibly cinnamon-flavoured, from wide glass goblets.

Another of the oddities of the dining room was the centre-piece on the table, which was *fixed*: a large silver sculpture showing Neptune waving his trident threateningly at the diners, while next to him Amphitrite* winked slyly at them. They were on a rock rising up in the middle of a silver basin surrounded by dolphins and sea monsters which, by means of a clockwork mechanism concealed in the central leg of the table underneath, would spout water from their mouths. It was certainly a sumptuous and lively piece – with the one drawback, however: that only tablecloths with a large hole in the middle – from which Neptune emerged – could be used (the edges of the hole were concealed with flowers or leaves). There were no sideboards in the room, but there were four large console tables with pink-marble shelves. The dominant colour in the room was pink – the marble, the *toilette** worn by the Princess in the large painting, as well as the upholstery of the chairs, which was modern but delicately nuanced.

The house in Santa Margherita was thus a kind of eighteenth-century Pompeii where everything had been miraculously preserved – always a rare thing, but almost unique in Sicily, which through poverty and neglect is the most destructive place on earth. I am not sure of the reasons for this *phenomenal* continuity: perhaps it's because my great-grandfather had to spend twenty years there, between 1820 and 1840, in a kind of house arrest imposed on him by the Bourbon Kings as a result of certain misdemeanours committed on the Marina.* Or perhaps it's because my grandmother took such a passionate interest in looking after the place. But I'm sure it's also partly due to Onofrio Rotolo, her administrator and the only one of his kind I have ever known not to be a thief.

He was still alive when I was going to Santa Margherita. He was a little gnome of a man, **tiny in size** with a very long white beard. He lived with his wife, who was incredibly large and stout, in one of the many apartments attached to the main house, but with a separate entrance. Marvellous tales were told of his care and attention to detail: whenever the house was empty, he would go round it every night holding a lamp to check if all the windows were closed and the doors bolted; he only allowed his wife to wash the valuable porcelain crockery; in my grandmother's time, after each reception he would go round and feel the screws under the cane chairs; **coming back after a few months' absence, my grandfather would find a shot glass of cognac covered with a bit of paper, still half full ("This has some value, Your Excellency, and I couldn't bring myself to throw it away");*** during the winter months, he would spend entire days directing teams of porters in cleaning and tidying the vast house down to its remotest corners. Despite his age and his elderly appearance, his wife was extremely jealous, and every now and then we would hear stories of furious rows between them when she suspected him of having paid too much attention to the charms of a young housemaid. I know as a fact that on more than one occasion he went to see my mother and gave her a good scolding over excessive expenditure – it goes without saying she ignored him and perhaps even sent him away with a flea in his ear.

His death coincided with the rapid and sudden decline of this most beautiful of country houses. May these lines I write here, which no one will read, be a tribute to his untarnished memory.

For a boy in the house at Santa Margherita, adventure did not only lie in the unexplored rooms or in the winding paths of the garden, but also in many single objects. Think what a source of wonderment the centrepiece of the dining table must have been! Or the *boîte à musique** found in a drawer – a large clockwork mechanism in which a cylinder covered with an irregular pattern of sharp points lifted miniature steel keys as it revolved, producing faint, minute melodies.

Then there were rooms with enormous cupboards made of yellow wood whose keys had been lost – not even Don Nofrio knew where they were, and that tells you everything. After much hesitation, a locksmith was called and the cupboard doors were forced open. Inside were supplies of bedlinen, dozens upon dozens of sheets and pillowcases, enough for a hotel (and, it should be said, in addition to the already extraordinary quantities of such items there were already in the cupboards we knew about). Others contained woollen bedspreads, covered with pepper and camphor, or table linen, damask tablecloths, small, large and enormous, and *all* with a hole in the middle. In between the layers of this household abundance small silk gauze bags had been placed, containing what were once lavender flowers and was now just dust. But the most interesting cupboard was the one which housed eighteenth-century stationery. It was slightly smaller than the others and was crammed full with enormous sheets of the finest-quality writing paper, quill pens, tied neatly together in bundles of tens, red and green *pains à cacheter** and very long sticks of sealing wax.

Also, there were the walks we took around Santa Margherita. The one we did most often was to Montevago, because the way was flat, just the right distance (around three kilometres both ways) and had a definite if unattractive destination: the village of Montevago itself.

There was also a walk in the opposite direction, along the main road towards Misilbesi. The route passed in front of a huge umbrella pine and then crossed over the Dragonara bridge, in the dense midst of an unexpectedly wild forest, which reminded me of Doré's illustrations to scenes from Ariosto,* which I used to gaze at in those days. Having reached Misilbesi (a roguish-looking place, the epitome of all the violence and trouble I used to think no longer existed in Sicily, until a few years ago I came across a certain turn in the road near Santa Ninfa, at a spot called Rampinzeri, that brought back a fond remembrance of Misilbesi's roguish appearance), which consisted of a crossroads baking under the hot sun and marked by an ancient post office, along with three dusty and deserted roads that looked as if they led to Dis* instead of Sciacca or Sambuca, we would usually return in the carriage, as we had long since exceeded the regulation seven kilometres set for a walk.

The vehicle would follow us at a walking pace, occasionally stopping so as not to overtake us and then unhurriedly catching up again, so alternating periods of silence – and also invisibility, when it was concealed by turns in the road – with the beating of hooves as it closed the gap.

In autumn our walks would take us to the vineyards of Toto Ferrara, where we'd sit on stones and eat the intensely sweet grapes with their spotted skin (grapes grown for wine, since at that time, 1905 to 1910, grapes cultivated for eating were hardly known in our parts). Then we would enter a dimly lit room: at the back, a burly-looking lad would be thrashing about wildly in a barrel as he tramped the grapes beneath his feet – their greenish juice ran out through a wooden chute, and the air was filled with a heavy scent of must.

"Dance, and Provençal song, and sunburnt mirth."*

But no, there was no mirth* about it – in Sicily there never was and never is when someone's at work. Here there are no women singing their *stornelli** as they harvest grapes, like they do in Tuscany – no feasts and songs and couplings accompanying the threshing, as happens in Livonia: all work is "'*na camurrìa*",* a blasphemous infringement of the eternal rest conceded by the gods to our lotus-eaters.*

On rainy autumn afternoons our walk was confined to the public gardens in Santa Margherita, on the northern edge of town, at the top of a steep slope overlooking the great valley which perhaps forms the main axis of Sicily running from east to west and is in any case one of its few notable geographical features.

My grandfather had given the park to the town. It was inexpressibly melancholy: a longish avenue lined with young cypresses and old holm oaks led to a featureless open space opposite a chapel dedicated to Our Lady of Trapani. In the middle of it was a flowerbed with red and yellow *cannæ*,* while to the left there was a kind of little domed pavilion or temple from where one could admire the view.

It was worth doing so. In front of you was an immense hillside completely covered in the yellow of harvested wheat fields, with occasional patches of burnt stubble giving it the appearance of a huge couched beast. On the flanks of this lioness or hyena (depending on the mood of the observer), you could hardly make out the villages against the background, because of their greyish-yellow stone buildings: Poggioreale, Contessa, Salaparuta, Gibellina, Santa Ninfa – oppressed by poverty, the torrid heat of the day and the darkness of night, which enveloped them without a single countering gleam of light coming from any of the houses.

On the chapel at the back of the gardens' central square were clear signs of the anti-clerical feelings of the local law students, who would now be home for the holidays. You would often find the verses from Carducci's 'Hymn to Satan' scrawled in pencil on its walls: "Hail thee, Satan, / you rebel god, / you avenging power / of reason".* And when my mother (who knew the 'Hymn to Satan' by heart and whose lack of admiration for the poem was based only on aesthetic grounds) sent Nino the gardener the following morning to whitewash over the mildly sacrilegious verses, two days later there duly appeared: "I excommunicate you, O Priest", "harbinger of grief and fury" and other such bitter rants which the worthy Giosuè had deemed necessary to direct against Citizen Mastai.*

On the steep rocky slope under the pavilion you could pick capers – and I regularly risked ending up with a broken nose in trying to do so. Apparently, it was also a place where you could find Spanish flies, whose heads, when crushed to powder, are such a powerful aphrodisiac. I was quite certain at the time that such insects were to be found there, but from whom I had the information, when I had it and why remain a mystery. Whatever the case may be, I've never actually seen a Spanish fly in my life, dead or alive, whole or crushed to powder.

These were the easy walks that could be done during the day. There were also longer and more complicated ones, or proper "excursions".

The "excursion" par excellence was the one to Venaria, the hunting lodge on top of a hill just outside Montevago. This was an excursion that was always undertaken as a group, about twice a year, and a certain air of comedy always accompanied its rituals. The decision was made: "Next Sunday we'll have lunch at Venaria" – and when Sunday morning came, we'd set off around 10, the ladies in a dog cart and the men on donkeys. Although all the men there – or nearly all of them – owned horses or at least mules, it was customary to ride donkeys: only my father objected, and had found a way of getting round the problem by declaring himself to be the only person capable of driving the dog cart* with its women passengers along the roads to Venaria. In the cages underneath the vehicle – which were supposed to house the dogs – bottles and cakes for the lunch were stored instead.

Full of banter and laughter, the band set off along the road to Montevago. In the middle of the dusty group was the dog cart, in which Mother, Anna (or "Mademoiselle", as the case might be), Margherita Giaccone and any other ladies in the party attempted to protect themselves from the dust by wrapping themselves in thick grey veils of almost Muslim impenetrability. Round about them capered the *scecche* (in Sicily donkeys are almost always referred to as female, like ships in English) with their flapping ears. Falls occurred: some of them authentic, some due to actual mutiny on the part of the donkeys, and some put on just to add a bit of colour. We went through Montevago, much to the vocal indignation of the local dogs, and once we reached the bridge at Dagali we would get off just below it and start the climb up the hillside on foot.

The avenue leading up the hill was magnificent: about three hundred metres long, it ascended in a straight line to the top of the hill between a double row of cypress trees. These were not immature cypresses like those at San Guido,* but hefty centenarians: from their thick foliage an austere fragrance wafted at every season of the year. The rows of cypresses were occasionally interrupted by large stone benches, and in one place by a fountain with a gargoyle still spouting water every now and then. So, in the fragrant shade, we would climb towards the Venaria up above, immersed in bright sunlight.

It was a late-eighteenth-century hunting lodge which was regarded as "teeny-weeny", but in reality must have had at least twenty rooms. Built on top of the opposite side of the hill from which we made our ascent, the view from it plunged down into the same valley that could be seen from the Villa Comunale, which from this greater height seemed even more desolate.

Here is the curious plan of the house.

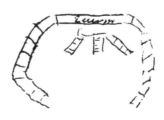

Our cooks had set out from Santa Margherita at 7 a.m. and already had everything prepared. When the boy on lookout announced our approach, the dishes containing the memorable *timballi di maccheroni alla Talleyrand** would quickly go into the ovens so that when we arrived there was barely time for us to wash our hands before going out onto the terrace, where two tables had been laid for us. Under an unsweetened papery crust of puff pastry, the pasta in the timbales was glazed with the lightest of sauces and steeped in the flavours of ham and truffles cut into match-thin strips.

The timbales were followed by huge portions of cold sea bass in mayonnaise, then by stuffed turkeys and mountains of potatoes. The digestive overload threatened to kill you off. That nearly happened for real once to big Giambalvo – but he was saved by a bucket of cold water on his face, followed by a prudent nap in a darkened room. The finishing touch was one of the ice-cream cakes which Marsala, the cook, knew how to make to perfection. The choice of wine, as always in abstemious Sicily, was unimportant. The guests did want to drink and demanded that their glasses should be filled to the brim ("Right to the top – no gap!" they would cry to the waiters) – but then they would only down one such glass, at most two.

As the sun began to set, we would start the return journey down the hill to Santa Margherita.

I've spoken of "excursions" but, on reflection, in actual fact the only "excursion" was the one to Venaria: in earlier years there were others, but I have only a vague memory of them – or rather, since "vague" is not the right word, it would be better to say that they are "hard to describe". The visual impression of them is still vivid in my mind, but it wasn't then connected to any words. For example, we went to Sciacca by carriage to have lunch with the Bertolino family when I was about five or six years old, but I have no memory at all of the lunch, of the people we met, or of the journey to get there. Of Sciacca itself, however – or rather of the cliff-top walk overlooking the sea – I have retained a photographically exact image, so that when I returned there two years ago for the first time in 52 years, I was easily able to compare what I was seeing – the many similarities and the handful of differences – with the scene I remembered.

My most distant memories are always in some special sense memories of "light". In Sciacca my image is of such a deep-blue sea it almost appears black, glinting fiercely under the noonday sun, and a sky misty with humidity, typical of high summer in Sicily – a railing running beside a sheer drop, and a kind of kiosk where there was a café (still there today) on the left as you gazed out over the waves.

The name of Cannitello, on the other hand, evokes a sky full of louring rain clouds. It was a small country house situated on a steep hill reached by a winding road. To get there, for some unknown reason, the carriage horses had to be driven at a gallop. I can see the landau with its blue cushions covered in dust from the road (the fact that they were blue shows that the vehicle was not our property but one we had hired) and, seated in the corner, Mother trying to comfort me, though she was terrified herself, while alongside us thin trees sped by like the wind, and the coachman's shouts combined with the cracks of his whip and the frantic jangling of the carriage bells (no, the vehicle was definitely not one of ours).

From the image I retain in my memory of the house in Cannitello, I can say that its appearance was aristocratic but very impoverished. At the time of course I wouldn't have been capable of such a socio-economic assessment, but I can confidently make it now that I examine the photograph I have just extracted from the archive of my memory.

I have spoken of the people who frequented the house in Santa Margherita, but I still have to describe the guests who came to stay with us for a few days or a few weeks.

The first thing to point out is that there were not many of them. There were no cars in those days – or, to be more precise, there may have been about three or four in the whole of Sicily, and the terrible state of our roads induced the owners of these *raræ aves* to use them only in the cities. Santa Margherita was then a twelve-hour journey from Palermo – and what a journey!

Among the guests I remember my aunt Giulia Trigona* with her daughter Clementina and her nursemaid, a skinny and austere German woman totally different from my two Annas. Giovanna (now Albanese) had not yet been born, and I've no idea where my uncle Romualdo* was – no doubt busy displaying his handsome person and his impeccable dress sense.

Clementina was a boy in girl's clothing, just as she still is today. She was forceful, brusque and ready to use her fists – and while these qualities turned out to be drawbacks later, they made her a good playmate for a six- or seven-year-old boy. I can clearly remember endless chases riding our tricycles, not only in the garden but also in the house, between the entrance hall and "Leopold's drawing room", a distance of about four hundred metres there and back.

I've already told the story of our transformation into monkeys in the cage in the garden. I also remember our breakfasts around the wrought-iron tables there, though I fear this may be a "fake" memory: a photograph survives of these breakfasts, and it is perfectly possible – as is often the case – that I am confusing the present memory of the photograph with a genuine memory from remote childhood.

I must say that I don't remember my aunt Giulia being present on these occasions: Clementina and I were probably still at the age when we ate our meals at a separate table.

* * *

On the other hand, I have an extremely vivid memory of **Giovannino Cannitello, the owner of the house I talked about earlier. His full name was Giovanni Gerbino-Xaxa,*** the baron of **Cannitello,** and he came from a good local family, sub-feudatories of the Filangeris, who had enjoyed the extremely rare and much envied right within their own feudal territories to invest two vassals in every generation as barons. The Gerbinos, who had been judges under the *mero et mixto* system,* had received this privilege – which is why my grandmother always used to refer to him as "first and foremost among all my vassals".

To my eyes Giovanni Cannitello looked like an old man, but he cannot have been much older than forty. He was extremely tall and thin and short-sighted: despite his glasses – a pair of pince-nez with extraordinarily thick and heavy lenses that must have been a torment to wear on the nose – he walked bent down in the hope of making out at least some shadow of the things that surrounded him. Indeed the poor man died blind not more than twenty years ago.

He was a kind and sensitive and well-loved man, if not very intelligent: he had devoted his life (and most of his wealth) to becoming a "man of elegance". As far as clothing was concerned, he had certainly succeeded: I have never seen such sober, understated and beautifully cut clothes as the ones he wore. He had been one of the numerous moths attracted by the bright lamp of the Florio family, ending up with burnt wings on the tablecloth after spinning around ecstatically for some time. He had been more than once with the Florios to Paris, even staying at the Ritz, and he had retained ever since a bedazzled memory of the city (of one aspect of it: its *boîtes*,* luxury brothels and girls for hire), which made him very similar to the above-mentioned Monteleone, with the difference that Dottor Monteleone's memories of Paris were all centred on the Quartier Latin and the École de Médecine. As it happened, Monteleone and Giovanni Cannitello did not get on at all well, perhaps precisely on account of their rival claims for the favours of the *Ville Lumière*.* A long-standing family joke used to tell the story of how Dottor Monteleone was once woken up in the middle of the night because **Cannitello** had attempted suicide by drinking a litre of petrol (a pretty chambermaid had rejected his advances), and merely turned over to go back to sleep, saying: "Push a wick down his stomach and light it."

Giovanni Cannitello (who, from the time of Mademoiselle Sempell onwards, was given the nickname "*le grand Esco*", from "*le grand escogriffe*")* was of a sentimental as well as amorous temperament. He attempted to take his own life on countless occasions (by means of a careful use of petrol or breathing in a brazier's fumes while keeping the window open) whenever rebuffed by the objects of his amorous attentions, usually from among the domestic staff.

He died almost entirely blind and completely penniless not many years ago (about 1932) in his house in Via Alloro, next to the Cocchieri church. Mother continued to visit him until he died, and would come back shocked at the way he was now so bent over that when he sat in an armchair his face was barely twenty centimetres from the floor. She had to sit on a cushion on the floor in order to converse with him.

In earlier years Alessio Cerda was also a frequent guest at Santa Margherita. Then he became blind and, although we still used to visit each other in Palermo, he never came again to Santa Margherita. There was a photograph of him wearing his uniform as a lieutenant of the Guide* in the ill-fated Italian army of 1866 – soft cap, soft boots, soft gloves: that same softness, in short, that led to our defeat at Custoza.* But I will speak of the highly idiosyncratic figure of Alessio Cerda later.

Another person who came to visit us once – in one of those early cars – was Paolo Scaletta. I think his visit was unplanned. He was travelling to some Valdina properties in Menfi, not far from Santa Margherita, when his vehicle broke down, so he came to us and asked if he could stay.

Many of my most crucial memories, pleasant or unpleasant, are linked to Santa Margherita.

It was at Santa Margherita that I was taught to read, at the untender age of eight. Before then I was read to: on alternate days – Tuesday, Thursday and Saturday – it was "Sacred History", a kind of compendium of the Bible and the Gospels, while on Monday, Wednesday and Friday there was… classical mythology. This way I acquired a solid familiarity with both these subjects: I can still tell you how many brothers Joseph had and what their names were, and I can find my way around the complicated family intrigues of the Atrides. Before I knew how to read for myself, my grandmother felt obliged, out of sheer good nature, to read Salgari's adventure novel *The Queen of the Caribbeans* to me for an hour – I can still see her trying not to doze off while she read aloud about the daring feats of the Black Corsair and Carmaux's braggadocio.*

Eventually it was decided that this vicarious transmission of religion, classical myth and high adventure could not continue, and I was entrusted into the care of "Donna Carmela", a teacher in the elementary school at Santa Margherita. Nowadays elementary schoolmistresses are pert and elegant young ladies who are keen to inform you about the educational methods of Pestalozzi and James,* and who ask that you address them as "Professoressa". In 1905, in Sicily, the schoolmistress in an elementary school was a little old woman, still largely a peasant, wearing glasses and a black shawl wrapped round her head. However, such women knew how to do their job perfectly: within two months I could read, write and spell words with double consonants and accented syllables* without a moment's hesitation. Entire weeks were spent in the so-called "blue room" – with a window onto the second courtyard, and just across the corridor from my bedroom, the "pink room" – taking down dictations syllable by syllable – or rather, "dic-ta-tions syll-a-ble by syll-a-ble" – and repeating over and over again, dozens of times, "*di, do, da, fo, fa, fu, qui* and *qua* NEVER have an accent". Thankful toil! – **since it means that, unlike a certain distinguished member of the Italian Senate, I will never be surprised to see how often, in newspapers and on posters, the word "*Reppubblica*" is erroneously spelt with two Bs.***

After I had learnt to write Italian, Mother started to teach me to write in French. As for speaking the language, I could already do this, since I had been to Paris – and to France in general – many times. But I learnt to read it at Santa Margherita. I can still see Mother seated with me at a desk as she wrote out slowly and in large letters "*le chien, le chat, le cheval*"* down the column of an exercise book with a shiny blue cover, informing me that "ch" in French is pronounced like the "sc" in "scirocco" and "Sciacca".

Torretta [fragment]

And then there was Torretta. As much as Santa Margherita was loved, Torretta was detested. It has always symbolized and accompanied illness and death, and for me continues to do so.

Torretta is a village around twenty kilometres outside Palermo, inland from the coast and about five hundred metres above sea level. Its lofty position gave it the reputation as a cool and healthy spot; in reality the place, hemmed in by a narrow valley, overlooked by steep and barren mountains on every side, and devoid of sewers, running water, a postal service and electricity, is one of the least healthy places on earth. Whenever any members of my family fell sick and were sent to Torretta to "recover", they wasted away, grew melancholy and within three months died. The local population were sullen, dirty, uncouth, and lived like rats among those sordid alleyways.

Our house was the "baronial residence" of the village, and as such was located on the main square – just as in Santa Margherita, but with a world of difference. There the square was spacious, tree-lined and sunny, and all the houses surrounding it were in at least decent condition; in Torretta it was narrow, dark and closed in: its cobblestones were always damp and adorned by the golden excrement deposited by the local mules. In the middle of it, there was an ugly rococo fountain with three wretchedly small spouts from which the only fresh water available in the village spewed forth; as a result it was surrounded day and night by a throng of women and boys holding their *quartare** in their hands, who, with a typically Sicilian scorn for any kind of order or waiting in line, created all sorts of scenes by shouting, jostling, trampling and threatening each other.

Our house was not small – five balconies proudly looked onto the piazza – but it seemed tiny compared to the one in Santa Margherita. It was unfortunate that the façade had not been painted in the usual cheerful Sicilian colours of white and yellow: it was in white with the window and balcony frames done in a darkish grey, more like a faded black, which gave the whole building the look of a tomb belonging to some noble family, displeasing precisely because it awoke foreboding.

Because of the ceaseless shouting and continuous commotion round the fountain, we lived in the rooms at the back of the house, which opened onto a terrace overlooking the valley, one of those bleak Sicilian valleys, bare and discordant, which always let you glimpse through an opening right at the end of them a tiny strip of bright-blue sea. On that side of the house, the air would have been good and complete calm would have reigned had it not been for the fact that about ten metres below the level of the terrace there was a large tank to which the women of Torretta, carrying their *cantari** on their shoulders, came the whole day long to empty out the excess contents of their cesspits, so that it was impossible to escape the smell of excrement in Torretta, whichever part of the house we were in.

Surrounded by these all-enveloping effluvial smells, the house in Torretta was entered via a large staircase consisting of two flights of steps which led to an entrance hall...

Joy and the Law

H E MANAGED TO ANNOY everyone when he got on the bus.

His briefcase bulging with other people's papers, the enormous parcel he was carrying, which meant he had to hold his left arm bent outwards, the grey woollen scarf wrapped round his neck, the umbrella on the point of unfurling – all this made it difficult for him to show his return ticket. He had to place the large parcel on the ledge of the conductor's till, which then spilt an avalanche of small coins onto the floor – and as he tried to bend down to pick them up, the people behind him, who were worrying their coats would get caught in the automatic doors because of the time he was taking, started to protest. He managed to squeeze himself into the row of passengers gripping the handrail: he was slight of build, but with everything he was carrying he took up more space than a nun wrapped in seven tunics. As the bus slid on its muddy way through the chaotic traffic, his inconvenient bulk provoked ill humour from one end of the bus to the other: he stood on people's toes and they stood on his, the other passengers scolded him, and when he heard someone behind him hiss a three-syllable word alluding to his presumed marital misfortunes,* he felt honour-bound to turn his exhausted eyes in that direction and throw what he liked to believe was a glare of angry defiance.

Meanwhile, the bus drove on through streets lined with façades in a rustic baroque style concealing an underlying degradation that contrived to spill out at every corner, past eighty-year-old shops lit by yellowish lamps.

When they reached his stop, he rang the bell and got off, tripped over his umbrella and finally found himself standing on the uneven kerb, in his own little space. After quickly reassuring himself that his plastic wallet was still in his pocket, he was free to savour the happiness he was feeling.

The wallet contained his end-of-year bonus – all thirty-seven thousand two hundred and forty-five lire of it – which he'd been handed just an hour before, and with it a temporary relief from a lot of thorny problems: his landlord, who was owed six months' arrears and was all the more importunate as the rent was at a fixed rate; the zealously punctual collector of the instalments owed on the purchase of that rabbit-fur jacket for his wife ("It suits you much better than a long cape, darling – it makes you look slimmer"); the angry looks from the fishmonger and the greengrocer. Those four large-denomination banknotes also put paid to the worries about the next electricity bill, the sorrowful glances at the state of the children's shoes, the anxious looks at the gas flame when it started to flicker. The money certainly didn't spell opulence – that was for sure – but it did mean there would be a reprieve in the struggle, which for the poor amounts to real happiness. And perhaps a couple of thousand lire would be left over for a brief moment before they too were consumed in the glow of Christmas dinner.

But he had received his end-of-year bonuses too many times before for him to confound the fleeting exhilaration they always induced with the rosy euphoria he could feel expanding within him now. Yes, rosy: the same colour, in fact, as the wrapping of the parcel that caused his arm to ache with its pleasant weight. The source of the euphoria filling him was right there: a fifteen-pound panettone he had brought from the office. Not that he was especially keen on this quality-assured yet dodgy concoction of flour, sugar, powdered eggs and currants – in fact, if truth be told, he didn't actually like it. But fifteen pounds of such a luxury all at once! Though a small thing, it was an immense bounty for a house where everything that came in was measured out in ounces and half-pints – a prestigious product for their larder filled with third-rate products! How happy Maria would be! The children would squeal with joy over the next fortnight as they explored this unknown Eldorado – a teatime treat!

But these were the joys of other people: material joys made of vanilla sugar and coloured paper – of panettone, in short. The happiness he was feeling was quite different: a spiritual happiness, a mixture of pride and tenderness – yes, his was truly a spiritual happiness.

Earlier that day his boss, the Commendatore, dispensing payslips and Christmas greetings with his ex-Fascist official's haughty bonhomie, had announced that the fifteen-pound panettone presented by a "Great Manufacturing Company" to their office would be given to the most deserving employee – therefore he had asked his dear colleagues to nominate on the spot, by democratic vote (these were his words), the lucky recipient.

The panettone sat in the middle of the desk, heavy, hermetically sealed, "heavy with ominous signs",* as the Commendatore himself might have said twenty years earlier in his Fascist uniform. A ripple of chuckles and murmurs had run through the assembled staff, and then all of them, his boss leading the way, had shouted out his name. It was really gratifying: it was such a reassurance on the safety of his position – it was, in short, a triumph. Nothing, later, could shake off this invigorating sensation: not the three hundred lire he'd had to pay to buy coffees all round for his friends at the local bar in the mingled garish rays of a stormy sunset and underpowered neon lighting, not the weight of the booty or the insults from his fellow passengers in the bus – nothing, not even the faint realization, deep down, that his colleagues might have chosen him, the most impecunious among them, out of a momentary feeling of patronizing pity. He was indeed too poor to allow the weed of pride to grow where it shouldn't.

He started to walk home, along a rundown street to which the Allied bombs fifteen years earlier had merely given the finishing touches, and reached a ghostly little square with a block of flats tucked away at the back like some lurking phantom.

He gave a cheerful greeting to the porter, Cosimo, who knew his own monthly pay packet was larger and therefore despised him. Nine steps, three steps, nine steps: he reached the floor where some Cavaliere lived. Ugh! It's true he had a Fiat 1100, but also a wife who was old, ugly and rude. Nine steps, three steps, a stumble, nine steps: some Dottore's apartment. Even worse! His good-for-nothing son was mad about Lambrettas and Vespas, and his waiting room never had any patients in it. Nine steps, three steps, nine steps: at last his small flat, the residence of a man who was well regarded, upright, respected, rewarded – an accountant at the top of his league.

He opened the door and slipped into the narrow hallway, already filled with the smell of fried onions. On a tiny bench no bigger than a basket he placed the ponderous packet, the briefcase stuffed with other people's concerns and his thick scarf. His voice rang out: "Maria! Come here! Just come and take a look at this beauty!"

His wife emerged from the kitchen. She was wearing a blue housecoat streaked with the soot from the pans: her small hands, reddened by dish-washing, were clasped over her stomach, now shapeless after various childbirths. The children, their noses dripping, were gathering around the monumental rosy-pink object and squealing with pleasure, not daring to touch it.

"Well done! And what about your pay packet? I haven't got a cent left."

"Here it is, darling. I'll just keep the small change, two hundred and forty-five lire. But look how stunning it is!"

Maria had been pretty once, up to a few years ago, with her wayward eyes lighting up an intelligent little face. But the arguments with shopkeepers had harshened her voice, the poor diet had coarsened her skin, the constant prospect of a future fraught with uncertainty and obstacles had dimmed the brightness of her gaze. What had survived in her was only a saintly and therefore unbending soul – a profound goodness lacking all tenderness and only capable of expressing itself by reproaches and prohibitions – together with a wounded and yet tenacious sense of class as the niece of one of Palermo's leading hat-makers, with a shop on Via Indipendenza. She despised the very different origins of her husband Girolamo: she adored him as one might adore a sweet-natured but dimwitted child.

She cast an indifferent glance at the decorated paper. "Good. We can send it tomorrow to Risma, the solicitor, to show our appreciation for what he's done for us."

Two years earlier, the solicitor had entrusted him with a complex bookkeeping job and, in addition to paying for it, had invited them both to dinner at his apartment, full of abstract art and metal furniture. The new shoes he'd bought especially for the occasion had caused him agony. And now, because of this lawyer who had all he needed and more, they – Maria, Andrea, Saverio, little Giuseppina and himself – had to give up the only lucky find they'd had in years!

He ran into the kitchen, grabbed a knife and immediately started to cut the gold ribbon that some industrious factory worker up in Milan had neatly tied round the wrapping of the panettone – but a reddened hand touched him wearily on the shoulder: "Don't be a child, Girolamo. You know we owe Risma a favour."

The Law had spoken – the Law promulgated by unsullied hat-makers.

"But, darling, I got it as a prize! It's a recognition for my work, a proof of how much they think of me!"

"Let's not talk about it. Sure, you've got such fine-minded colleagues… Girì,* they were just being charitable, that's all it was." She used the old affectionate diminutive as her eyes – in which only he could still see the gaze which had once enchanted him – looked smilingly at him.

"Tomorrow you'll buy a small panettone – that'll be enough for us. We'll get four of those red corkscrew candles we saw in Standa.* We'll have a real party."

So the following day he bought a small anonymous panettone, two rather than four of those remarkable red candles, and sent the Christmas giant off to Dottor Risma by courier, which cost him a further two hundred lire.

In addition, after the Christmas holidays, he was obliged to purchase a third panettone. He had to take it – sliced up so they wouldn't be able to see the difference – to his colleagues in the office, who had teased him for not bring-ing them even some crumbs from the magnificent prize he'd carried off home.

The fate of the primeval panettone was shrouded in mystery.

Girolamo returned to the courier office – "Lightning Express" – to ask what had happened to it. He was shown, with an air of contempt, the register of receipts, which the solicitor's housekeeper had signed – on the back. However, after the holidays were over, a visiting card arrived in the post: "With thanks and festive greetings".

Their honour was still intact.

The Siren

I N THE LATE AUTUMN OF THAT YEAR, 1938, I found
myself in a state of fully fledged misanthropy. I was living
in Turin, and "*tota** No. 1", as she was going through my
pockets to find a fifty-lire note while I was still asleep, had
come across a billet-doux from "*tota* No. 2". Despite its
numerous spelling mistakes, it left no room for reasonable

doubt as to the exact nature of our relationship.*

My awakening was sudden and stormy. The little apartment in Via Peyron resounded with colourful vernacular
expletives. An attempt was also made to scratch my eyes out
– which I was only able to ward off by giving a slight twist
to the dear little creature's left wrist. This act of entirely
legitimate self-defence brought an end to the outburst – but
also to the idyll. She quickly got dressed, threw a powder
puff, lipstick, hanky into her handbag, together with the
fifty-lire note (*causa mali tanti*),* and, with the forceful
declaration, repeated three times, that I was a *porcanun*,* left.
She had never looked so pretty as she did during her fifteen-
minute fit of fury. I watched her leave from the window and
disappear into the morning mist – tall, slender, triumphant
in her newly reacquired elegance.

I never saw her again – just as I never saw a black cash-
mere pullover I had paid an arm and a leg for, which had

the unfortunate advantage of being designed for both men and women. She had left, on the bed, two twisted hair clips, of the kind known as "invisible".

That same afternoon I had an appointment with No. 2 in a tea room on Piazza Carlo Felice. At "our" table – a small round one in the west corner of the second room – I found not the chestnut curls of the girl I was more than ever hoping to see, but the weaselly face of her twelve-year-old brother Tonino, just finishing a cup of hot chocolate with a double helping of whipped cream. As I approached, he stood up with the customary urbanity of people from Turin: "*Monsù*, Pinotta's not coming. She told me to give you this note. *Cerea, monsù.*"* And with that he took his leave, not forgetting to take the two brioches that were still on his plate. The creamy-white card informed me that our separation was permanent – a result of my perfidy and my "dishonest Southern ways". It was clear that No. 1 had tracked down and set No. 2 against me – so that I was now left standing in the middle.

Over the course of twelve hours I had managed to lose two girls who had complemented each other usefully in so many ways, as well as a pullover which I was particularly fond of. I also had to pay the bill for that wretched boy, Tonino. My (very Sicilian) sense of self-esteem had been wounded: I'd been made a fool of – so I decided to retire for a certain period of time from the world and all its vanities.

* * *

I couldn't have found a more appropriate place to spend this period of retreat than the café in Via Po where I used to go, solitary as a bear, whenever I could – and always in the evening, after I'd finished work at the newspaper. It was a kind of Hades peopled by the bloodless shades of retired army colonels, magistrates and university professors. In a dim light – during the day because of the outside portico and the cloudy sky, and at night because of the enormous green lampshades – these simulacra would play at draughts or dominoes. No one ever raised his voice, no doubt for fear that too loud a sound might cause his weak apparition to disappear. It was a very convenient limbo.

Like the creature of habit I am, I always went to the same corner table carefully placed in such a way as to cause the maximum discomfort to the customer who sat there. On my left, ghostly figures of ex high-ranking army officers played at tric-trac with a couple of phantoms formerly of the Court of Appeal: the dice thrown in this confrontation between the military and legal professions would roll out of the leather cup with a muffled rattle. On my right* always sat a very elderly gentleman, wrapped in an old overcoat with a threadbare astrakhan collar. He read foreign magazines all the time, smoked Tuscan cigars and frequently spat. Every now and then he would close one of his magazines and gaze into the coils of smoke as if searching for some lost memory.

Then he would resume his reading and spitting. He had very ugly hands, knobby and reddish, with the not always clean fingernails cut straight. Once he came across a photograph, in one of his magazines, of a Greek statue from the archaic period – one of those in which the eyes and the nose are far apart and the lips have an ambiguous smile – and I was surprised to see his misshapen fingertips caress the image with an almost aristocratic delicacy. He saw that I had seen him, grunted angrily and ordered another espresso.

Our relations might have remained at this level of latent hostility had it not been for a chance occurrence. I used to bring with me from the office copies of six or seven daily newspapers, including on one occasion the *Giornale di Sicilia*. Those were the years when the MinCulPop* reigned supreme and all the newspapers were identical. That issue of Palermo's newspaper was even more banal than it usually was, and nothing distinguished it from the ones published in Milan or Rome, except for the bad quality of the printing. I read it through quickly and pushed it aside on the table. I had just started looking through yet another of MinCulPop's manifestations when the man spoke to me: "Excuse me, sir. Would you mind if I took a look at your *Giornale di Sicilia*? I come from Sicily, but I haven't seen a newspaper from there for over twenty years." He had an extremely cultivated voice and spoke with an impeccable accent: his old grey eyes looked at me with deep detachment.

"Of course, please do. I'm from Sicily myself. If you'd like, I could easily bring you the paper every evening."

"Thank you, but I don't think that will be necessary. I am simply curious to look at it. If Sicily is still like what it was when I lived there, I don't suppose there's anything good to report – as for the past three thousand years."

He skimmed the pages, folded the paper and handed it back to me, then plunged into reading a pamphlet. When he rose to leave, he was obviously intending to beat a retreat without having to say goodbye, but I got up and introduced myself. He murmured through clenched teeth some name I didn't catch, and didn't give me his hand to shake, but when he reached the door he turned round, lifted his hat and bellowed out: "Bye for now, compatriot!" He disappeared under the portico, to my amazement and the muttered disapproval of the ghosts at their games.

I performed the magic rites that were necessary to call forth a waiter and, pointing at the empty table, asked him: "Who was that gentleman?"

"*Chiel?*" came the reply. "*Chiel l'è 'l senatour Rosario La Ciura.*" *

Even as a journalist, with my superficial, gappy knowledge, I'd heard the name. As the most distinguished Greek scholar of his time, he was one of a handful of Italians who enjoyed a universal, undisputed reputation. Now I understood his thick journals and the reason he had stopped to caress that illustration, as well as his brusque manners and secret refinement.

The following day, in the office, I went through that curious file containing the obituaries that are still "pending". There was one for La Ciura – not too badly done, for once. It described how the great man had been born at Aci Castello in the province of Catania, to a poor lower-middle-class family – how, thanks to an astonishing aptitude for Greek and through a series of scholarships and learned publications, he had obtained the chair of Greek Literature at the University of Pavia at the age of twenty-seven, subsequently being called to the chair in Turin, where he had remained until retirement. He had given a series of lectures in Oxford and Tübingen and travelled extensively: appointed a senator before the Fascists came to power and a member of the Lincean Academy,* he had received honorary doctorates from the universities of Yale, Harvard, New Delhi and Tokyo – as well as, of course, from the most famous European universities, from Uppsala to Salamanca. The list of his publications was prodigiously long: many of his works, especially those on Ionian dialects, were considered essential reading – it is enough to say that he had been the only foreign scholar invited to edit the Teubner* edition of Hesiod, with an introduction in Latin of unsurpassable scientific depth. His crowning glory was that he was not a member of the Accademia d'Italia.* What had always distinguished his writings from those of the other scholars in his field, erudite as they were, was his vivid, almost carnal sense of classical antiquity. This can be seen in a collection of his essays in Italian entitled *Of Gods and Men*, which was judged to be a work not only of the highest scholarship, but also of living poetry. He was, in short, in the final words of the obituary, "an honour to his fatherland and a universal beacon of culture". He was seventy-five years old and lived decorously, if not opulently, with his pension and his allowance as a senator. He was unmarried.

It's useless to deny it: we Italians, the legitimate sons (or fathers) of the Renaissance, regard the Great Humanist as a being superior to all others. The opportunity of finding myself in daily contact with the highest representative of this refined, almost necromantic and largely unprofitable science flattered and troubled me. I experienced the same emotions a young American might feel on being introduced to Mr Gillette:* awe, respect and a very particular form of not ignoble envy.

That evening, when I made my descent into Limbo, I was in a very different mood from previous days. The senator was already seated at his table and replied to my respectful greeting with a barely audible mumble. When he had finished reading an article and jotting down notes in a small notebook, he turned to me and said in a strangely musical voice: "Compatriot, from the way you greeted me I can tell that one of the anaemic denizens of this place must have told you who I am. Forget it and, if you haven't done so already, also forget the aorist tenses you learnt at school.

Instead, tell me your name, since yesterday you muttered something when you introduced yourself – and, unlike you, I can't ask anyone your name, since I'm sure no one here has the faintest idea who you are."

He spoke with a haughty aloofness: it was evident that in his eyes I was less than an insect, perhaps one of those motes of dust which float about pointlessly in beams of sunlight. And yet his tranquil voice, his precise language, his use of the familiar "*tu*" in addressing me, suggested the serene exchange of a Platonic dialogue.

"My name is Paolo Corbera.* I was born in Palermo, where I graduated in law. I'm now working here for *La Stampa*. And just to reassure you, Senator, I should add that I scraped through the Greek exam in my school-leaving certificate with a mark of 5+. I believe the plus was only added to make sure I got an overall pass."

He gave a half-smile. "Thank you for telling me – it's better that way. I hate talking to people who think they are knowledgeable when in fact they are ignorant, like my university colleagues. If truth be told, they only know the external forms of Greek, its peculiarities and deformities. The living spirit of the language so foolishly called 'dead' has never been revealed to them. In fact, nothing has ever been revealed to them. But they are unfortunate wretches: how could they ever have felt the living spirit of Greek if they've never had the chance of hearing it spoken?"

Now it may be true that pride is preferable to false modesty, but it seemed to me that the senator was somewhat exaggerating. Indeed, the thought occurred to me that in his old age he had gone slightly soft in the head, exceptionally intelligent as that head was. Those poor devils, his colleagues, had had the chance to hear ancient Greek spoken as much as he had – in other words, never.

He went on: "Paolo… you've had the good fortune to be named after the only apostle who had some culture and a smattering of literary taste. Girolamo would have been better, though. The other names you Christians give your children are beneath contempt. They're all the names of slaves."

This disappointed me: he came across as the usual anticlerical academic with an added dash of fascism *à la* Nietzsche. Was that possible?

He continued to speak with that winning musicality in his voice and the energy of someone who had perhaps not spoken for a long time. "Corbera… Am I deceived or isn't that one of the most important Sicilian names? I remember my father paying a small annual rent for our house in Aci Castello to the administrator of the Corbera family of Palina or Salina, I can't remember which. He used to joke every time he had to pay, and said that if there was one thing certain it was that that handful of lire would never end up in the pockets of the "holder of the right of the lord", as he used to put it. So do you belong to that family or are you the descendant of some peasant who just adopted his master's name?"

I confessed that, yes, I was one of the Corberas of Salina – indeed their last surviving scion: all the splendours and all the sins, all the uncollected rents and unpaid duties – in short, all the various stratagems a Leopard uses to adapt* – had converged in me and me alone. Strangely, the senator seemed pleased by the news.

"Very good. I have a lot of respect for the old families. They possess a memory – a miniscule one, it's true – but still better than what all the rest have. In terms of the attainment of physical immortality, they represent the best your kind can achieve. Get married soon, Corbera, since people of your kind haven't discovered any better method to ensure survival than scattering your seed in the most unlikely places."

I was decidedly losing patience with him. "People of your kind." Whose kind? The entire low-born herd of us who didn't have the good luck to be Senator La Ciura? And had he achieved "physical immortality"? Looking at his wrinkled face and stout body, you wouldn't have said so...

"Corbera of Salina," he continued, undeterred. "You mustn't take offence if I continue to address you using '*tu*', as I do with my immature students, who are only young for a brief moment."

I told him that I was not only honoured but pleased he addressed me that way – which was true. After these preliminary formalities, we turned to the subject of Sicily. Twenty years had passed since he had set foot on the island – and the last time he'd been down there (he spoke like someone from Piedmont) he had stayed for only five days, in Siracusa, in order to discuss with Paolo Orsi* certain issues about the alternation of semi-choruses in performances of classical drama.

"I remember they wanted to drive me from Catania to Siracusa. I agreed only when I learnt that the road at Augusta goes inland, whereas the train goes along the coast. Tell me about our native island. Even though it's populated by asses, it's a beautiful land. The Gods resided there – perhaps during those endless Augusts they still do. But don't speak to me about those few temples that were built recently – you wouldn't know the first thing about them anyway, I'm quite sure."

So we talked about Sicily's eternal aspect – its natural beauties: the fragrance of rosemary on the Nebrodi mountains,* the taste of Melilli's honey,* the May wind swaying the fields of harvest wheat as seen from Enna, the solitary places round Siracusa, the aromatic gusts from citrus orchards that are said to waft over Palermo at sunset on certain days in June. We spoke of the enchantment of certain summer nights in the bay of Castellammare,* when the stars are mirrored in the sleepy waves of the sea and the gazer stretched out among the lentisk bushes feels his spirit rapt in the vortex of the sky above him, while his body – tense and alert – fears the approach of demons.

The senator had hardly ever been back to Sicily in the last fifty years, but he had preserved peculiarly vivid memories of small details.

"The sea... the sea in Sicily is the most colourful and romantic sea I've ever seen. That'll be the only thing you won't be able to spoil – outside the cities, I mean. In the seaside restaurants do they still serve those *rizzi*,* covered in spines and cut in half?"

I assured him you could still find them, though few ate them now for fear of catching typhus.

"But they're the most wonderful thing you have down there, with their blood-red cartilage, like a woman's genitals, fragrant with the smell of salt and seaweed. Typhus my foot! If they're dangerous, then they're dangerous like everything the sea gives, which can lead to death or immortality. When I was in Siracusa with Orsi, I insisted we ate some. What a taste, what a divine thing to look at! It's my most wonderful memory from the last fifty years!"

I was puzzled and fascinated that such a man felt free to use metaphors which were little short of obscene and could display a childish greed for sea urchins – which after all don't taste that special.

We went on talking for a long time – and when he rose to go, he insisted on paying for my coffee in that peculiarly tactless way he had ("It's a well-known fact that young men from good families never have a penny to their name"), and we parted like friends, if you discount the age difference of half a century and the thousands of light years that separated our cultural backgrounds.

We went on meeting each evening. My misanthropic fervour against humanity had started to abate, yet I made sure I never missed making my descent into the infernal regions of Via Po in order to see him. Not that we spoke a lot: he continued to read and take notes, and only turned to address me from time to time – but when he did, it was always with the same harmonious and fluent combination of pride and insolence, mixed with the most varied allusions and sudden gleams of mysterious poetry. He also continued to spit – and I eventually realized he did so only when he was reading. I think he too had developed a certain fondness for me, though I'm under no illusions about his feelings: if it was indeed fondness, then it wasn't the sort "my kind", to use his expression, can feel for a fellow human being, but resembled what an old spinster might feel for her budgerigar. As she talks and complains to it, she knows perfectly well it's a mere uncomprehending bundle of feathers – but were it not there, she would miss its presence. And indeed I started to notice that whenever I arrived slightly late the old man's haughty gaze would be staring at the door.

It took about a month for our conversation to move from general remarks – though always, in his case, of striking originality – to the more indiscreet topics that distinguish the talk between two friends from that of mere acquaintances. I made the first move. His habit of spitting annoyed me (as it had the owners of the Hades we frequented, who had ended up positioning a gleaming brass spittoon next to his table), so one evening I asked him if he shouldn't be taking better care of his persistent catarrh. I put the question without thinking, and immediately regretted asking it: I waited for the ceiling to fall on my head at the explosion of the senator's ire. Instead, in his usual measured tones, he replied: "My dear Corbera, I don't suffer from catarrh. With your acuteness of observation, you should have noted that I never cough before spitting. My spitting has nothing to do with illness – on the contrary, it's a sign of my mental good health. I spit from sheer disgust whenever I come across some ridiculous absurdity in my reading. If you cared to examine that object (he pointed to the spittoon), you would find in it very little saliva and not a trace of mucus. I spit for symbolic and nobly cultural reasons: if you don't like it, go back to your native drawing rooms, where spitting is frowned on only because nothing is ever capable of causing disgust."

The extraordinary rudeness of his reply was mitigated only by the abstracted look in his eyes. Nevertheless, I felt like getting up and walking out on him – but luckily I took a moment to think and realized the fault lay with me and my impertinent enquiry. I didn't leave, and the senator immediately counter-attacked: "And what about you, may I ask – how come you frequent this Erebus full of shades and, as you have just pointed out, catarrhal emissions – this point of convergence for failed lives? There's no shortage in Turin of the kind of creatures men like you find attractive.

An outing to the hotel in Castello, a trip to Rivoli, or to the baths at Moncalieri, and you could easily enjoy the dirty diversions you're looking for."

I couldn't help laughing at hearing him so well informed about the places frequented by pleasure-seekers in Turin.

"But how do you know about these places, senator?"

"I know about them, Corbera, I know about them. If you frequent the corridors of power – political and academic – you find out about them. In fact, it's all you find out about. But please believe me, the sordid pleasures that people of your kind indulge in have never held the slightest interest for Rosario La Ciura."

It was evident the senator spoke the truth: his demeanour and his words bore the unequivocal mark (as they used to say back in 1938) of a sexual reserve that had nothing to do with the fact he was elderly.

"To tell you the truth, senator, I started to frequent this place precisely to get away from the world for a while. I'd got into a bit of trouble with a couple of the 'creatures' you've just, rightly, condemned."

Without mincing his words, he retorted at once: "Cuckolded, Corbera, eh? A venereal disease?"

"Neither of those. Actually, worse than that. They left me." And I told him about the ridiculous events that had taken place two months earlier. My account could afford to be facetious now, since the wound to my self-respect had healed over in the meantime. Anyone else other than that damned Greek expert, listening to my unhappy tale, would have either pulled my leg about it or, less likely, felt sorry for me. Instead, that formidable old man did neither: he grew indignant.

"That's what you get, Corbera, when sick, squalid creatures start coupling. I'd say exactly the same about you to the two young trollops, were I ever to have the displeasure of meeting them."

"But they weren't sick at all – they were both in tip-top form. You should have seen what they put away whenever we went to dine at the Specchi. And they weren't squalid either: you couldn't have seen a more magnificent couple of females – really elegant too."

The hiss of the senator's disgusted spit could be heard. "They were sick, I tell you. Fifty or sixty years from now, perhaps a lot sooner, they'll die, and, if that's the case, then they were sick from the beginning. And squalid too – wearing trinkets, stealing pullovers, trying to imitate the simpering actresses they've seen in the cinema – you call that elegance? So it was noble generosity of spirit which led them to riffle through their lover's pockets for greasy banknotes instead of giving him, like others, rosy-pink pearls and branches of coral? But what can you expect from women like that – mutton dressed as lamb? Doesn't it disgust you – them and you – rolling your carcasses around in rank and sweaty sheets?"

Dazed, I replied: "But the sheets were always clean, senator!"

He exploded in fury: "And what's that got to do with anything? I'm talking about the stink of corpses, your corpses.

I repeat, how is it possible to dally with people like them, people of your sort?"

I already had my eyes on a sweet little adventurous *cousette*,* so I took offence. "So you think you can only take blue-blooded princesses to bed?"

"Who's talking about princesses? They'll end up as dead meat, like all the rest. But I'm wrong to talk about such matters to you, young man – you won't understand. It's your destiny – you and your little friends – to end up in the mephitic swamps of your filthy pleasures. Only a few, a very few, are capable of understanding."

With his eyes gazing at the ceiling, he smiled, his face filled with a rapt expression, then he shook my hand and left.

I didn't see him again for three days. On the fourth day I received a telephone call in the office. "*L'è monsù Corbera?** This is Bettina speaking, the housekeeper for Senator La Ciura. He's asked me to tell you he has had a bad cold, but is feeling better now and would like to see you this evening after dinner. Please come to Via Bertola, No. 18, at nine o'clock. We're on the second floor."

The summons, abruptly broken off, allowed no time for reply.

No. 18 Via Bertola was an old, run-down block, but the senator's apartment was huge and well kept – thanks, I imagine, to the constant cares of Bettina. The parade of books began in the entrance hall – ordinary-looking, inexpensively bound books like all those found in real working libraries. Thousands more volumes could be seen in the three rooms I was led through. In a fourth room sat the senator, wrapped up in a large dressing gown of the finest, softest camel hair I had ever seen. I found out later that it was made from the precious wool of some Peruvian animal and was a gift from Lima's Academic Senate. He didn't get to his feet when I entered the room, but greeted me warmly. He was better, in fact completely well, and planned to be out and about again as soon as the current spell of freezing weather had released its grip on Turin. He offered me a glass of resinous Cypriot wine, sent to him by the Italian Institute in Athens, some really disgusting pink *lokums*,* supplied by the Archaeological Mission in Ankara, and some rather more reasonable local pastries, thoughtfully provided by the sensible Bettina. He was in high good humour: he even grinned broadly, twice, and apologized for his outburst a few days before in the Hades of Via Po.

"I realize, Corbera, that I may have expressed myself somewhat extravagantly – though my meaning was as sober as could be, believe me. Let's not think about it."

I hadn't in fact given any further thought to it: on the contrary, I felt full of respect for the old man, who I suspected was, despite his triumphal career, deeply unhappy. He gobbled down the repellent *lokums*.

"Sweets should taste of sugar and nothing else, Corbera. As soon as you try to add other flavours, they become like perverse kisses."

He gave sizeable crumbs to a large boxer called Eacus, who had wandered in at some point.

"For those who can understand such things, Corbera, this creature, ugly as he is, resembles the Immortals far more than your grasping little hoydens."

He refused to show me his library. "It's all classical stuff, which couldn't possibly interest someone like you, who flunked his Greek exam at school, morally speaking."

But he showed me round the room where we were sitting, which was his study. There were only a few books in it: among them I noticed the collected plays of Tirso de Molina, *Undine* by la Motte Fouqué and the play of the same name by Giraudoux – as well as, to my surprise, the works of H.G. Wells.* But on the other hand the walls were covered with large full-scale photographs of archaic Greek statues – not the normal kind of photographs any of us can buy, but images of superlative quality which had quite clearly been specially requested and solicitously provided by museums all over the world. They were all there, those magnificent creations: the "Rampin Horseman" from the Louvre, the "Seated Goddess" originally from Taranto and now in Berlin, the "Warrior" from Delphi, the "Kore" from the Acropolis, the "Apollo of Piombino", the "Lapith Woman" and the "Phoebus" from Olympia, the world-famous "Auriga of Mozia"… The room was filled with the glow of their ecstatic and ironic smiles – the exultance of the way they held their serene, proud poses.

"You should frequent these, Corbera, not your little *tote*."

The mantelpiece was lined with ancient vases and bowls: one showed Odysseus tied to the mast of his ship and the Sirens throwing themselves off a cliff onto the rocks below to punish themselves for letting their prey escape. "Silly stories, Corbera, just silly petit-bourgeois stories made up by the poets: no one manages to escape the Sirens – and even if they did, they wouldn't kill themselves for such a trivial matter. Besides, how on earth could they ever succeed in killing themselves?"

On a small table, in an ordinary-looking frame, there was an old and faded photograph: a young man of about twenty, almost naked, with a thick shock of tangled hair and a joyful expression on his exquisitely beautiful face. Perplexed, I paused a moment in front of it: I thought I understood. But no. "And this, compatriot, this was and is and shall be for ever" – he stressed these words – "Rosario La Ciura."

The poor old senator wrapped up in his dressing gown had been, in his youth, as beautiful as a god.

Our conversation turned to other topics, and before I left he showed me a letter, written in French, from the Rector of the University of Coimbra, inviting him to become a member of the honorary committee of a conference on Classical Greek studies that would take place in Portugal in May.

"I'm very pleased. I'll take the boat from Genoa, the *Rex*, with all the other people going to the conference from France, Switzerland and Germany. Like Odysseus I'll block my ears so that I won't have to listen to all those halfwits rabbiting away, and I'll spend my time enjoying the voyage: the sun, the blue sky, the smell of the sea."

As he escorted me out of the room, we passed the bookcase where the works of H.G. Wells were shelved, and I decided to risk mentioning to him how surprised I'd been to see them there.

"You're right, Corbera, they're quite awful. One of them's a novelette which if I ever happened to reread it would make me want to spit for a month on end. Now that would really scandalize a well-brought-up drawing-room poodle like you, wouldn't it?"

After my visit, our relations grew decidedly cordial, at least on my side. I made elaborate plans to order a supply of sea urchins, as fresh as possible, from Genoa. When their arrival on the following day was confirmed, I managed to buy a bottle of white wine from the slopes of Mount Etna and some coarse peasant bread, and timorously invited the grand old man to visit me in my small flat. To my great relief he accepted the invitation gladly. I went to fetch him in my Balilla* and brought him to Via Peyron, which is more or less out in the sticks. He was an anxious passenger and had absolutely no confidence in my skills as a driver.

"I know now what you're like, Corbera. If we're unlucky enough to come across one of your hoydens in a short skirt, you're quite capable of turning round to look at her and we'll both end up squashed flat against a wall." But we didn't encounter any such freak of nature wearing a short skirt and worth looking at, so we arrived in one piece.

For the first time since I'd known him I saw the senator laugh out loud: it happened when I showed him my bedroom.

"So this is the stage of your lewd adventures, Corbera!"

He looked at the few books I possessed. "Well, well. You're perhaps less of an ignoramus than you appear to be. Now here's someone" – he added, holding up my copy of Shakespeare – "here's someone who had some grasp of things. 'A *sea-change into something rich and strange.*' – '*What potions have I drunk of Siren tears?*'"*

When the dependable Signora Carmagnola came into the drawing room carrying the tray with the plate of sea urchins, lemons and the other things, he was ecstatic.

"What? How extraordinary that you thought of these. How did you ever guess they're what I crave more than anything else?"

"You need have no worries about eating them, senator: this morning they were still in the sea off Liguria."

"That's just like you and your kind. You're always the same, decadence and putrescence forever in attendance, always listening out for any signs of Death slowly getting nearer. Poor wretches! But thank you, Corbera, you've been a real *famulus*.* A pity they weren't picked from our seas and wrapped in our algae. You can be sure no god ever pricked himself and bled on these spines. You've certainly done your best, Corbera, but you could say these are sea urchins from Boreal climes, found dozing on the cold rocks of Nervi or Arenzano."*

For people from Milan, going to the Ligurian coast is like visiting the tropics, but it was evident the senator was one of those Sicilians who regard it instead as an extension of Iceland. The sea urchins were cut in two, revealing the curiously partitioned and bleeding flesh within. I'd never noticed it before, but the senator's bizarre comparison made me see that the inside was really very much like a cross section of some delicate female organ. He ate them greedily, but gave no signs of pleasure as he did so: he was concentrated, almost sorrowful. He refused to squeeze any lemon juice on them.

"That's typical of you and your kind, always wanting to combine flavours. The sea urchin should also taste of lemon, sugar should also taste of chocolate, love of paradise!"

When he'd finished eating, he drank a sip of wine and then closed his eyes. After a while I noticed two tears trickle out from beneath his wrinkled eyelids. He stood up, walked over to the window and circumspectly wiped his eyes. Then he turned back to me.

"Have you ever been to Augusta, Corbera?"

I had done three months of my military service there:* during our off-duty hours two or three of us would go off in a boat, sailing the clear waters of the bay.

He was silent, and then, in an irritated tone of voice, asked me: "And did you and your fellow squaddies ever go to the small enclosed bay above Cape Izzo, behind the hill overlooking the salt ponds?"

"We certainly did. It's the most beautiful spot in the whole of Sicily: the *dopolavoristi** haven't found out about it yet. Do you remember how wild that stretch of the coastline is, senator? Completely empty, not a house in sight. The colour of the sea is peacock-blue – and right opposite you, across the ever-changing waves, there's Mount Etna. That's the finest view of Etna, from there: serene, powerful, really godlike. It's one of those places in Sicily where you glimpse the island's eternal aspect – its real nature, which it's been mad enough to turn its back on. The pasture where the cattle herds of the Sun God roam – that's what Sicily's really supposed to be."

The senator didn't speak at first. Then: "You're a good lad, Corbera. If you weren't such an ignoramus, something might have been done with you." He came up to me and kissed me on the forehead. "Go and fetch that tin box you drive around in. I'd like to go home."

Over the following weeks we continued to see each other. We took to going on nocturnal walks, usually down Via Po and across Piazza Vittorio, with its air of a military parade ground, to watch the rapidly flowing river and the Collina* behind – that spot where a touch of fantasy is injected into the city's otherwise rigid geometry. It was the beginning of spring, that affecting season of doomed youth. The first lilacs were coming into blossom on the riverbank, pairs of impatient lovers with nowhere else to go stretched out on the still-damp grass.

"Down there the sun is already hot, the algae are flowering – you can glimpse the sudden gleams of fish in the moonlit water as they swim up to the surface on clear nights. And we're here, instead, watching this characterless and empty stretch of water, standing in front of these barrack-like buildings lined up like soldiers or monks in procession, listening to the gasps of dying lovers as they couple." But the thought of the voyage to Lisbon cheered him up: the day fixed for his departure was getting nearer. "It'll be enjoyable. You should come too. It's a pity it's not a trip for those whose Greek is not up to scratch. You and I could talk in Italian, but if you got your irregular optative verbs wrong with Zuckmayer or Van der Voos you'd be done for. Though you probably know more than they've ever done about what it really means to be Greek – not because of your learning, of course. By a kind of animal instinct."

Two days before he left for Genoa he told me that he would not come to the café on the following day, but wanted me to call on him at home at nine o'clock in the evening.

The ritual was the same as on the previous occasion. The three-thousand-year-old Gods filled the room with their youthful radiance like a stove sending out heat. The gaze of the godlike young man in the faded photograph taken fifty years before seemed to look out with dismay at the sight of his metamorphosis into the white-haired old professor slumped in a chair.

When we'd drunk our glasses of Cypriot wine, the senator summoned Bettina and told her that she needn't stay up. "I'll escort Signor Corbera out when he leaves. Now, Corbera, I've asked you here for a purpose, at the risk of spoiling whatever plans you had for some fornicatory rendezvous in Rivoli, because I need you. I'm leaving tomorrow, and when you go travelling at my age you never know whether you'll ever come back, especially when it's a sea voyage. I've become fond of you, you know – your naivety is touching, and your transparent animal scheming amusing. And then, it seems to me that you combine the senses and reason in a sort of synthesis, as a few of the best kind of Sicilians manage to do. It's only right therefore that I don't leave you unsatisfied, without any explanation for some of my oddities, some of the remarks I've made to you – which I'm sure will have seemed to you like those of a madman."

I protested, feebly: "It's true I haven't understood many of the things you've said, but if I didn't, I thought it was due to the limitations of my mind, not to an aberration of yours."

"It doesn't matter, Corbera, it's all the same. The old always seem quite mad to the young, though often the reverse is true. However, in order to explain properly, I need to tell you about something unusual that happened to me, when I was 'that young gentleman there'" – and he pointed to the photograph. "We need to go back to 1887, which will seem like prehistory to you, but most certainly isn't for me."

He got up from the chair behind his desk and came to sit beside me on the sofa. "Forgive me, I'll need to talk quietly. The important words must never be shouted. You'll only find 'love's cry' (or hate's) in cheap melodramas or among the uneducated classes – which is the same thing. So then: in 1887 I was twenty-four years old. I was the young man you can see in the photograph. I had a degree in Classical Studies and I had already published two short articles on Ionian dialects which had caused quite a stir in my university. For over a year I'd been preparing the exam for a chair at the University of Pavia. Furthermore, I had never slept with a woman. In fact I have never slept with a woman either before or after that year." I could have sworn that my face was a mask of marble-like immobility, but I was mistaken. "It's coarse of you, Corbera, to blink like that. I've told you the truth, and it's a truth I'm proud of telling you. I know that we men from Catania have a reputation – justifiably so – for being capable of getting our wet nurses pregnant, but I was the exception. When you spend all your time, day and night, as I did then, in the company of gods and demigods, you don't have much desire to tramp round the brothels in San Berillo.* Besides, in that period, religious convictions also restrained me. Corbera, you really should try to control that blink of yours: you give yourself away all the time. Yes, I said 'religious convictions'. I also said 'in that period'. I no longer have any – not that that's made any difference, at least in that regard.

"A slacker like you, Corbera – after all, you probably got your job at the newspaper by asking a Party official to pull strings for you – can't have any idea what it means to prepare for an examination for a chair in Classical Greek Literature. You need to work flat out for two years, almost driving yourself mad in the process. Luckily, I already knew the language well, indeed as well as I know it today – and I'm not saying this just for the sake of it. It was all the rest – the Alexandrian and Byzantine variants in the texts, the extracts quoted, always inaccurately, by Latin authors, the endless literary connections with mythology, history, philosophy, science... It can drive you mad, as I've said. So I was working like a dog and, in order to pay the rent for my lodgings, at the same time I was also giving private tuition to students who'd flunked their school exams. I was living only on black olives and cups of coffee. On top of all this, that summer of 1887 – which was a hellishly hot one as every now and then happens down there – there was

that other big catastrophe. Every night Etna erupted, as if
regurgitating all the heat of the sun it had had to absorb
during the fifteen hours of day. If you happened to touch a
balcony railing at noon, you needed to be taken to the near-
est hospital. The basalt paving stones felt as if any moment
they'd return to their original molten state. And almost
every day there was a scirocco wind which blew round you
like the clammy wings of some bat. I was at the end of
my tether, but a friend rescued me. He bumped into me in
the street while I was wandering along completely dazed,
stammering lines of Greek verse I was no longer capable
of understanding. My appearance worried him. 'Rosario,
if you stay here you'll go out of your mind – and that'll put
paid to the exam. I'm just about to leave for Switzerland'
– he came from a wealthy family – 'but I've got a cottage
in Augusta – it's just three rooms, a long way outside the
town, only twenty yards from the sea. Pack a bag, take
your books with you and go and spend the summer there.
Come round in an hour's time and I'll let you have the key.
The atmosphere'll be completely different there, you'll see.
When you get to the station, ask for the Carobene cottage
– everyone knows it. Promise me you won't think twice
about it: leave this evening.'

"I took his advice and left that very evening, and the next
day when I woke up I saw out of the window not the toilet
waste pipes that used to greet me from the opposite side of
the courtyard at dawn, but a calm pure sea stretching before

me and a now unthreatening Etna, shrouded in morning mists, in the far distance. The place was completely deserted – as you told me it still is – and quite astonishingly beautiful. The cottage was in bad repair, and the only furniture in its rooms was the sofa on which I slept, a table and three chairs, while in the kitchen there were some earthenware cooking pots and an old oil lamp. Behind the house there were a fig tree and a well. It was paradise. I went into the village and found the peasant who worked the Carobene land. I arranged for him to bring me, every two or three days, some bread, pasta and vegetables, and some oil for the lamp. I had brought olive oil with me, some of my family's olive oil which my poor mother used to send me in Catania. I rented a small boat from a local fisherman – he came over with it in the afternoon – together with a fish trap and a hook. I decided to stay for at least two months.

"Carobene was right: everything was different there. The heat of the day was still intense, but there were no walls for it to reflect off: it didn't reduce you to a state of animal stupor, but induced a kind of relaxed euphoria. The sun no longer ruthlessly roasted you alive, but became a genial – if still brutal – provider of energy, as well as a magician who studded every fold and crest of the sea with movable diamonds. It no longer cost me any effort to study: as I lay gently rocking in the boat for hours on end, the books I was reading no more seemed like obstacles I had to conquer, but became keys opening doors to an entire world: one of its most fascinating aspects was right in front of me. I would often chant poems aloud – and the names of all those gods that most people have forgotten or have never even known about once more floated across the waves of the ocean, which once had grown stormy or calm at the mere sound of them.

"I lived in complete solitude, broken only by the visits of the peasant who brought me my provisions every three or four days. He never stayed for more than five minutes: seeing my excitement and my wild looks, he must have thought I was about to go mad. And it's true that the sun, the solitude, the nights spent under the circling stars, the silence, the very scant food and the study of remote subjects all combined to weave a kind of enchantment round me, as if I were waiting for some wondrous event to occur.

"Which duly came – at six o'clock in the morning on the fifth of August. I had not been long awake and immediately got into the boat. With a few pulls on the oar I swung away from the pebbly beach and stopped beneath a large rock. In its shade I could shelter from the sun, which was already swelling with splendid rage and transforming the pale morning sea into a mass of blue and gold. I was declaiming poetry when I felt the edge of the boat suddenly dip, on the right, behind my back, as if someone in the water had gripped it in order to climb in. I turned and saw her: the smooth face of a sixteen-year-old girl emerging from the water, her two small hands holding on to the side of the boat. She was smiling – her pale lips were slightly parted to show small teeth, pointed and white, like those of a dog. But it wasn't anything like one of the smiles you see on the faces of your kind, always adulterated with some other kind of emotion – benevolence, irony, pity, cruelty or what have you – it expressed only itself, in a kind of animal joie de vivre, an almost godlike happiness. Her smile was the first of a series of spells that affected me, revealing the existence of serene, forgotten heavens. The water was dripping down her tangled sun-coloured hair into her green, wide-open eyes, streaming across her pure, childlike face.

"However prepared our reason might be for a wondrous event, when one occurs it gathers all its shadowy forces against it and tries to explain it away with the memory of run-of-the-mill events – so, as anyone else would have done, I thought she was a swimmer and stepped carefully to where she was, bent down towards her and stretched out my hands to help her climb in. But, with a gesture of amazing vigour, she lifted herself straight out of the water as far as her waist, clasped her arms round my neck, enveloping me with an unknown fragrance, and slid into the boat. From the waist down she had the body of a fish, covered in tiny blue and mother-of-pearl scales, ending in a forked tail that beat slowly against the bottom of the boat. She was a Siren.

"Lying on her back, she tucked her hands behind her head and, with a serene lack of shame, displayed the delicate hairs underneath her armpits, her breasts splayed slightly apart, her perfect stomach. From her rose what

I've clumsily called a fragrance, a bewitching marine aroma, youthful and euphoric. We were in the shade, but just twenty yards from us the sea shimmered with delight under the sun. I was almost naked and could barely conceal my arousal.

"She spoke, and so I sank even deeper under a third and even stronger enchantment, after that of her smile and her smell: her voice. It was slightly guttural and thick, with innumerable overtones: behind the actual words you could hear the undercurrents moving leisurely through the sea in summer, the rustle of far-flung foam across a sandy beach, the breeze ruffling the tidal waves. There's no such thing as the song of the Sirens, Corbera: they hold us captive with their voice alone.

"She spoke Greek, and I had great difficulty in understanding her. 'I heard you speaking by yourself in a language like mine. I like you, I am yours. I am Ligeia, Calliope is my mother.* Don't believe the fables that are told about us: we never kill anyone, we only love.'

"I was rowing the boat, bent over her and staring into her smiling eyes. We reached the beach. I took her aromatic body in my arms, and we moved out of the brilliant sunlight into thick shade. As I carried her along, she was already filling my mouth with a kind of ecstasy that, compared to human kisses, is like the finest wine compared to insipid water."

The senator was telling me his story in a low voice. I had always tacitly compared my own numerous sexual adventures with what I assumed to be his rather more limited experiences in the field, which stupidly made me feel less inferior to him. Now I felt humiliated. Even when it came to love-making, I was for ever and unreachably out of his league. Not for one moment did I think he was spinning me a yarn – even the most sceptical listener would have acknowledged the unmistakable note of veracity in his voice.

"So began the three weeks we spent together. It's not appropriate – and it wouldn't be kind to you – to enter into details. It's enough to say that in our embraces I experienced the highest state of spiritual ecstasy together with the most basic form of physical pleasure, without a trace of any social resonance – like the solitary joys our mountain shepherds feel in sexual congress with their goats. If the comparison disgusts you, it's only because you're incapable of moving from the animal level to the superhuman one: in my case both levels were merged.

"Do you remember what Balzac wanted to express but didn't dare to in 'Une Passion dans le désert'?* Ligeia's immortal limbs gave off such a life force that the energy consumed in the act was never depleted – on the contrary, it increased. During those three weeks, Corbera, the intensity of my love-making equalled the experiences of a hundred of your Don Giovannis over an entire lifetime. And what love-making! Safe from cloisters and crimes, untouched by a Commendatore's rancour or the paltriness of a Leporello,* remote from all the sentimental demands, the fake sighs and

false swoons that unfailingly mar your miserable kisses...
It's true a Leporello did once appear on the scene – he
disturbed us on the very first day, but never came back.
About ten o'clock I heard the sound of the peasant's boots
as he approached down the path to the sea. I managed
just in time to throw a sheet over Ligeia's unusual body
as he appeared in the doorway. When he saw the part that
remained uncovered – her head and neck and arms – this
Leporello obviously thought I was having an illicit fling and
suddenly displayed a new respectfulness. His visit was even
briefer than usual and, before he took himself off up the
path, he gave me a sly wink with his left eye, while his right
thumb and index finger curled an imaginary moustache at
the corner of his mouth.*

"I've said we spent twenty days together, but you mustn't
think that during those three weeks we lived 'like husband
and wife', as they say, sharing bed and board and doing
everything together. Ligeia often went away. Without a
word of warning, she'd dive into the sea and disappear,
sometimes for hours on end. When she came back it was
almost always in the early morning. She would either come
to the boat if I'd gone out in it, or if I was still in the cottage
drag herself on her back along the pebbled beach, half-in
half-out of the water, calling to me to come and help her.
She called me 'Sasà', using the familiar form of my name,
which I'd told her. As I went to pick her up, hampered as
she was by the part of her body which in the water allowed

her to move so fluently, she looked like some wounded animal – an impression completely dispelled once I'd gaze into her laughing eyes.

"She only ate live creatures. I often watched her emerge from the waves, her delicate torso gleaming in the sun, her teeth biting into a still-flapping silver fish – the blood would run down her chin and, after she'd taken a few morsels, she would throw the chewed-up cod or seabream behind her. She'd give a childish shout and clean her teeth with her tongue as the fish sank in the water, staining it with blood. I once gave her some wine to drink. She couldn't drink from a glass, so I poured a little into her tiny and slightly greenish palm. She lapped it up, making clucking noises like a dog, while her eyes filled with surprise at the unknown taste. She told me it tasted good, but she never accepted the offer to drink some again. Sometimes she would swim up to the beach with her hands full of oysters and mussels. I struggled to open the shells with my knife, whereas she broke them with a pebble and sucked out the palpitating flesh, together with bits of the shell, which didn't bother her at all.

"As I've already said, Corbera, she was an animal – and at the same time an Immortal. It's unfortunate that human speech cannot express all the time this synthesis in the way she expressed it, with utter simplicity, in her own body. And it wasn't just in carnal intercourse that she showed a joyfulness and delicacy entirely alien to the dark urgings of an animal in heat. Her way of speaking had a force and directness that I have only found again in a few great poets. Not for nothing was she Calliope's daughter. She was entirely uncultivated, knew no wisdom and dismissed any moral restriction with scorn – nevertheless, she was part of the source from which all culture, all learning, all morality springs, and she could express this primeval superiority in words of unadorned beauty. 'I am all, because I am merely the current of life as it flows unimpeded. I am immortal, because all deaths – from that of the cod I ate earlier to that of the great Zeus himself – flow into me and are gathered together in me, no longer as single determinate lives, but freely now as part of universal life.' Then she'd say: 'You are young and handsome. You should come with me to the sea. That way you will never know sorrow or age. You would live where I live, under the high sea mountains, dark and still: their native silence is so profound that we who live there are not even aware of it. I have loved you: remember, when you are tired, when you feel you cannot go on any more, all you need to do is to come to the sea and call me. I shall always be there, because I am everywhere, and your longing for sleep will be satisfied.'

"She told me about her life in the depths of the sea, the bearded tritons, the blue-green caverns, but she added that these too were mere foolish illusions: true reality lay much deeper, in the unseeing, soundless palace of the eternal and formless watery depths, where no light ever gleamed nor the slightest whisper was ever uttered.

"Once she told me she would be gone for a long time and only return on the evening of the following day. 'I must go far away, to a place where I know I'll find a present for you.'

"And she did indeed return holding a marvellous branch of purplish-red coral encrusted with shells and sea lichen. I kept it in a drawer for a long time, and each evening I would kiss where I remembered the fingers of the Indifferent One – that is to say, the Beneficent One – had rested. One day Maria, the housekeeper who was Bettina's predecessor, stole it in order to give it to her pimp. I later found it again in a jeweller's shop on the Ponte Vecchio,* stripped of its sacred aura, so cleaned and polished that I hardly recognized it. I bought it back, and when night came I threw it into the Arno: it had passed through too many profane hands.

"She also told me about the many human lovers she had had over the millennia of her adolescence: fishermen and sailors from Greece, Sicily, Arabia, Capri – some shipwreck survivors too, adrift and clinging to sodden spars. She had appeared to them amid the thunder and lightning of the tempest, transforming their dying groans into cries of ecstasy. 'They all followed my invitation: all came back to find me again – some immediately, others after what was, for them, a long time. Only one of them I never saw again. He was a beautiful boy with pure white skin and red hair. We made love together on a faraway beach where our sea flows into the great Ocean. He smelt of something stronger than that wine you gave me the other day. I think he never came back to me, not because he was happy with his life – of that I'm quite certain – but because when we met he was so drunk he couldn't understand a thing. He must have thought I was just an ordinary fishwife.'

"Those weeks of high summer sped by like a single morning. When they were over, I realized that in reality I had lived through centuries. This lascivious young girl, this cruel little animal, had also been to me the wisest of Mothers. With her presence alone, she had uprooted beliefs and dissolved metaphysics; her fragile and often bloodstained fingers had pointed the way to the realms of true eternal repose, as well as to the practice of an asceticism embraced not out of renunciation, but because it was impossible to accept other, inferior pleasures. I have certainly no intention of becoming the second man to disobey her call – I shall not refuse this pagan Grace which has been granted to me.

"The violent heat of that summer meant that it could not last long. Shortly after the twentieth of August, the first clouds timidly appeared in the sky, and some drops of rain, warm like blood, fell. All night, along the distant horizon, silent flashes of lightning followed slowly one after another, as if a god were pursuing some train of thought. In the morning the dove-grey sea, traversed by a secret restlessness, moaned like a dove; in the evening, though there was no breeze, the surface would become agitated, dappled with ever-changing but always soft hues – smoke-grey, steel-grey, pearl-grey – which seemed kindlier than the brilliance of the previous weeks. Distant wisps of mist could be seen over the water: perhaps on the Greek coast the rain had already arrived. Ligeia's mood too changed from its earlier brilliance to an affectionate grey. She spoke less and less, and spent hours stretched out on a rock gazing at the troubled horizon; she did not go away much. 'I want to remain with you. If I went into the sea now, my companions would keep me from coming back. Can you hear them calling to me?' And sometimes I really thought I could make out among the high-pitched squeals of the gulls a low sound – glimpse a sudden commotion in the water darting between rocks. 'They're sounding their conches, they're calling Ligeia to join them to celebrate the coming storm.'

"The storm overtook us at dawn on the twenty-sixth. From the rock we watched the wind whipping the far waters to a frenzy as it approached, while near us the sea heaved in huge, lazily moving, leaden-grey swells. The violent gust of wind was soon upon us, whistling in our ears, bending the parched stems of rosemary. The sea beneath us broke into waves: the first rolled forward covered in white foam. 'Goodbye, Sasà. You won't forget.' The breaker crashed against the rock, the siren threw herself into the iridescent spray. I didn't see her fall: it seemed to me she dissolved into the foam."

The senator left the next day. I went to the station to see him off. He was his usual grumpy and sarcastic self, but, when the train started to pull out, standing at the window he stretched out his hand to caress my head gently with his fingers.

On the following day, at dawn, the newspaper received a telephone call from Genoa. During the night, Senator La Ciura had fallen from the deck of the *Rex*, bound for Naples, and although lifeboats had immediately been lowered, his body had not been found.

A week later, his last will and testament was opened. Bettina had been left the money in his bank account and the furnishings of the apartment; his library was bequeathed to the University of Catania; in a recent codicil I had been left the Greek bowl with the painted figures of the sirens and the large photograph of the "Kore" from the Acropolis.

I sent both objects to my house in Palermo. Then the war came, and while I was in Marmarica* surviving on half a litre of water a day, the "liberators" bombed my house. When I was finally able to return, I found night-time looters had torn the photograph into strips to use as torches. The bowl was in smithereens. The largest fragment showed the feet of Ulysses, tied to the mast of his ship. I still have it. The books were deposited in the basement of the University building. Since there is no money available for shelving, they are rotting away slowly.

The Blind Kittens

DRAWN ON A SCALE OF 1:5000, the plan of the landed property belonging to the Ibba family filled a large sheet of waxed paper two metres long and eighty centimetres high. Not everything shown on the map belonged to the family. First of all, there was in the south a narrow strip of the sea coast laced with tunny-fishing nets that was no man's land. Then to the north there were inhospitable mountains where the Ibbas had never wished to poke their noses. But above all, around the lemon-yellow mass designating all the territory owned by the family, there were still numerous patches of white: land belonging to wealthy owners which they could not hope to acquire; land which had been offered to them but they'd turned down because of its poor quality; land they definitely wanted, but whose owners were still not tender enough to be chewed up properly. And then there were a very few areas that had once been yellow and had since returned to being white, because they'd been sold off in lean years, when there weren't enough peasants to work the land, in order to acquire other, better ones. But despite these patches, all at the edges, the extent of yellow was still imposing. Within this mass there was an oval-shaped nucleus round Gibilmonte: from there a broad branch extended eastwards – at first narrowing, then widening out again and stretching out two tentacles, one going in the direction of the sea and covering a short span of the coast, the other heading north and stopping where the steep, barren slopes of the mountains began. Westwards the expansion had been even greater: these were estates formerly belonging to the Church, and the Ibbas had advanced with the speed of a landslide and as easily as a knife cutting through butter. The two small villages of San Giacinto and San Narciso had been reached and encircled by deploying the light infantry of compulsory purchase orders. The defensive line formed by the Favarotti river had held out for a long time, only to give way and allow, as of today, 14th September 1901, the establishment of a bridgehead into the territory beyond the river with the acquisition of Pispisa, a small but succulent feudal morsel on its right bank.

On the plan the newly acquired property had not yet been coloured in with yellow, but the Indian ink and the fine brush had been set out on the writing bureau ready for Calcedonio, who was the only person in the household who knew how to do the job properly. Ten years ago, on the occasion of the expropriation of Sciddico, Don Batassano* Ibba, the head of the family and a near-baron, had tried to do it himself, with disastrous results: a large puddle of yellow ink spilt out over the entire map, and he'd had to pay out a large amount of money to get it redrawn. The bottle of ink, though, was still the same. Don Batassano had learnt his lesson and was content to gaze, with his impudent peasant's eyes, on the area to be coloured in and to reflect that it would now be possible to make out the land belonging to the Ibbas on a map of the whole of Sicily – no larger than a flea, of course, when seen against the immensity of the island, but still clearly visible.

Don Batassano was feeling satisfied but also irritated: two states of mind which frequently co-existed in him. The way the agent for the Prince of Salina, Ferrara* – who had arrived from Palermo in the morning to draw up the deed of sale – had nitpicked right up to the moment of signing the document! Not just to the moment of signing: even after! He insisted on being paid in banknotes – eighty of the large pink notes* issued by the Bank of Sicily – instead of the credit note that had been prepared for him, which meant he had had to go upstairs and extract the wad of notes from the innermost secret drawer in his writing desk – anxious all the time lest Mariannina and Totò might be around, as was perfectly possible at that time of day. It was true that the agent had allowed himself to be gulled over the annual fee of eighty lire payable to the Church Fund, for which he'd agreed to give up one thousand and six hundred lire of capital value, while Don Batassano (and his notary) knew perfectly well that their liability had been redeemed nine years earlier by another agent working for the Salinas.* But this didn't matter: even the most minimal opposition to what he wanted – especially when it concerned money – exasperated him: "They've no option but to sell, and even with their backs against the wall they still have a bee in their bonnet about being paid in banknotes rather than a credit note!"

It was only four o'clock, and there were still five hours before dinner. Don Batassano opened the window onto the narrow courtyard. The heavy stale heat of the September day spread into the darkened room. Down in the courtyard an old moustached man was preparing a game for the children of the master's family, smearing birdlime onto sticks made from reeds.

"Giacomino, saddle the horses – mine and yours. I'm coming down."

He wanted to go and inspect the damage done to the drinking trough in Sciddico. He'd been informed in the morning that some brats had broken one of the basin's quoins. The crack had been patched up as best it could be by using the gravel and the mud and straw you always find around a watering place, but the tenant, Tano, had asked for it to be properly repaired as soon as possible. More bother, more expense – it was endless! And if he didn't go and assess the damage himself, the workman hired to mend it would send in an exorbitant bill. He checked that the holster attached to his belt had the heavy Smith & Wesson in it: he was so used to going round with the gun that he no longer noticed whether he was carrying it or not. He went down the back slate stairs to the courtyard. The *campiere* was finishing saddling the horses. To mount his horse, Batassano used three brick steps attached to the wall for that purpose. He took the whip a boy was holding out to him and waited for Giacomino to mount his horse (without the help of the steps reserved for the master's use). The warden's son opened the ironclad gates to the courtyard, letting the afternoon light flood in, and Don Baldassare Ibba rode out with his bodyguard beside him onto the main road in Gibilmonte.

The two rode almost side by side, with Giacomino's horse just half a head's length behind his master's. The warden had his double rifle resting across the saddle bow with the iron-shod butt on one side and its two burnished barrels on the other; the animals' horseshoes struck, out of time with each other, on the pebbles of the steep roads. The women were spinning in front of their doors: they didn't greet them. Every now and then Giacomino would shout "Watch out there!" when a naked child was just about to roll under the horses' hooves. The archpriest of the village was sitting astride a chair with his head resting on the church wall and pretended to be asleep – after all, the benefice didn't belong to filthy-rich Ibba, but to the hard-up and faraway Santapaus. Only the *brigadiere*,* standing on the balcony of the Carabinieri station in his shirt sleeves, leant forward to greet them. They left the village and started to climb the track leading to the watering place. A lot of water had leaked away overnight and lay in a large puddle round the trough, where, mixed with clay, bits of straw, cow dung and urine, it gave off a sharp smell of ammonia. But the improvised repair had worked well: the water was no longer running out in the crack between the stone slabs of the trough, but was merely seeping out slowly, and the thin flow of water from the rusty pipe made up for what was lost through the leak. Don Batassano's satisfaction that the repair had cost him nothing led him to overlook the fact it was merely a temporary repair.

"What was Tano going on about, for Christ's sake? The trough is fine. It doesn't need anything doing to it. Tell the dickhead to learn to stand up for himself and not allow the first snotty-nosed kid who walks by to damage my property. And if he doesn't feel up to it, get him to find their fathers and send them to you for a good talking-to."

As they were returning, a frightened rabbit suddenly ran across the path, and Don Batassano's horse took fright and kicked out. The great man might have had a fine English saddle, but his stirrups were just pieces of rope looped back, and he was tumbled to the ground. He wasn't hurt – and Giacomino, used to the procedure, took hold of the mare's bridle and held her still as Don Batassano, standing by her side, angrily struck out with his whip, hitting her muzzle, ears and sides as she kept shivering and foaming. He concluded his lesson with a kick in the stomach, then he remounted and the two men continued their journey home as dusk began to fall.

Ragionier* Ferrara, in the meantime, hadn't realized the master of the house had gone out. He entered the study and, finding it unoccupied, sat down for a moment to wait. In the room there was a rack holding two rifles and a bookcase containing a few files (with written labels stuck to brown cardboard: "Taxes", "Title deeds", "Sureties", "Loans"); on the writing desk was the deed of sale that had been signed two hours earlier and, on the wall behind the desk, the map.

Ferrara got up to take a closer look. Thanks to his circle of professional acquaintances and the innumerable indiscretions he had heard, he was very familiar with the epic tale of how this vast extent of real estate had come into existence – the cunning, the lack of scruple, the defiance of the law, as well as the inexorability, the luck and the daring which had gone into its formation. He thought it might be interesting to colour the map differently, in the manner of schoolbooks which show the expansion of the House of Savoy's dominion across the peninsula by shading each successive acquisition with a different colour. The earliest possession had been Gibilmonte, where Don Batassano's father, Gaspare, an illiterate genius, had inherited around 1,600 square yards of land, a quarter of an acre of vineyard and a small three-bedroomed house. While still very young, he had seduced the deaf-mute daughter of a "bourgeois" family, small – very small – landowners only slightly less poor than Gaspare himself, and with the dowry from this forced marriage had managed to double his possessions. His physically impaired wife was quick to play her own part in her husband's plan: sordid cheeseparing enabled them to accumulate a little nest egg that was invaluable in a place like Sicily, where economic activity was at the time based exclusively on the practice of usury, as in the ancient city-states.

Shrewdly calculated loans – to people who had assets but not sufficient income to repay the interest – were made. The wordless moaning of Marta, Gaspare's wife, as she went on her weekly rounds at sunset to demand payment, became proverbial: "When Marta comes round with her dumbshow, it's time to pack up and go." After ten years of Marta's gesticulating visits, ten years of filching wheat from the Santapau estates on which Gaspare worked as a sharecropper, ten years of stealthily moving boundaries, ten years of satisfying their hunger, the couple's property had increased fivefold. Gaspare was just twenty-eight then, while Don Batassano was seven. There was a bumpy patch when the judicial authorities under the Bourbons took it into their heads to investigate one of the corpses it was customary to come across in the countryside. Gaspare had had to leave Gibilmonte, and his wife gave out that he had gone to stay with a cousin in Adernò in order to learn the skills necessary for the cultivation of mulberries – in actual fact, there wasn't an evening when, from the nearby hills, Gaspare had not gazed with affection at the smoke rising from the kitchen hearthside of his happy home. After that, the Thousand landed,* the world turned upside down, inconvenient documents conveniently went missing from the public registry offices, and Gaspare Ibba was able to make an official homecoming.

Things went on even better than before. Gaspare devised a strategy of sheer reckless genius: just as Napoleon at Austerlitz* dared to leave his centre undefended and reinforced his wings to close in on the hapless Austro-Russian army, so Gaspare mortgaged up to the hilt all the land he had fought so hard to acquire and, with the few thousand lire he made from the operation, arranged an interest-free loan to the Marquis of Santapau, who had landed in a tight spot due to his generous support of the Bourbon cause. As a result, after two years, the Santapaus had lost the feudal territory known as Balate* – which, as it happened, they had never even seen and believed, from the name, not to be fit for cultivation – the mortgages on the Ibba properties had been paid off, Gaspare had become "Don Gaspare" and the family had mutton for dinner on Saturdays and Sundays. Once the first hundred thousand lire had been reached, everything proceeded like clockwork: Church lands, acquired by paying the first two instalments on a miserably low estimated selling price, were obtained for a tenth of their real value; small groups of houses, together with the springs round which they'd been built and the rights of way they enjoyed, made the purchase, at a cut-price cost, of the surrounding land in the hands of lay owners extremely straightforward; the large aggregate income made it possible to purchase or expropriate landed property which was farther away.

When he died at what was still a young age, Don Gaspare already owned a considerable amount of land, but like Prussia in the middle of the eighteenth century, it consisted of large islands separated from each other by property belonging to others. Gaspare's son and heir, Baldassare, like Frederick II* before him, was entrusted with the glorious task of first unifying all the Ibba territories in one undivided block, and then extending the boundaries of the block towards yet more distant regions. Vineyards, olive and almond groves, pasturelands, rents from hereditary leases and, above all, arable land, were annexed and absorbed: the income from them poured into the modest study in the house in Gibilmonte, never staying there long, but soon emerging again, almost intact, to be transformed into yet more landed property. An unfailingly fair wind blew the good ship Ibba ever onwards – the name began to be uttered in reverential tones in every corner of the impoverished island. In the meantime Don Batassano had got married, at the age of thirty – not to a physically impaired woman like his venerated mother, but to a healthy eighteen-year-old by the name of Laura, the daughter of the local notary. The dowry she brought her husband comprised her own robust state of health, a respectable amount of money, her father's valuable legal experience and a willingness to submit to Batassano entirely, as long as her not inconsiderable sexual demands were satisfied. The arrival of eight children demonstrated the degree of submission she could achieve. An austere and unilluminated happiness reigned in the Ibba household.

Unusually for a Sicilian, Ragionier Ferrara was a man of tender heart. His father had been employed as an administrator by the Salina family during the stormy times of the old prince Fabrizio.* He himself had grown up in the protected atmosphere of the dynastic residence, and from force of habit wished only to lead a placid if mediocre existence. He was satisfied with having his own little piece of princely cheese to gnaw away at. He had the soul of a rodent, and the sight of those two metres of wax paper repelled him with their evocation of the grim determined struggles of a born carnivore. It reminded him of the instalments of that *History of the Bourbons of Naples* by La Cecilia* which his father, a fervent liberal, used to buy for him every Saturday – except that here in Gibilmonte there was no trace of the orgies which were supposed to have taken place in the palace at Caserta, as described in the book. Everything here was harsh, affirmative, puritanically unwholesome. He suddenly felt afraid and left the room.

At the family dinner that evening everyone was present apart from the eldest boy, Gaspare, who was in Palermo supposedly preparing to retake the exams for the school-leaving certificate (he was already twenty years old).* The meal was served with a rustic lack of refinement: all the cutlery – which was heavy and expensive – was piled in the middle of the table, and everyone fished whatever they needed out of the heap. The servants Totò and Mariannina obstinately persisted in serving the diners from the right. In her ripe plumpness, the Signora Laura was the very image of health at its flourishing pinnacle: her well-shaped chin, her delicate nose, her eyes gleaming with the tried-and-trusted pleasures of conjugal life were almost buried in folds of fat – fresh, firm and inviting. The outsize forms of her body were sheathed in black silk, as a token of continually renewed mourning. Her sons, Melchiorre, Pietro and Ignazio, and her daughters, Marta, Franceschina, Assunta and Paolina, sat round the table in a curious sequence of alternating resemblances, strangely combining their father's rapacious features with the compassionate looks of their mother. No attention at all had been paid to the clothes they were dressed in, either for the boys or the girls; the latter wore dresses of printed cretonne fabric, grey on white, while the boys were all in sailor suits – even Melchiorre, the oldest among those present, whose nascent adolescent moustache gave him the curious air of being an actual member of His Majesty's Navy. The conversation – or rather the dialogue between Don Batassano and Ferrara – consisted exclusively of two subjects: the price of land around Palermo as opposed to the land in the vicinity of Gibilmonte, and gossip about the capital city's aristocratic families. Don Batassano regarded all of them as being "down on their uppers" – even those who, only taking their collections of antiques into account, let alone their income, were as wealthy as he was. Almost never venturing beyond Gibilmonte, except for rare visits to the provincial capital and even less frequent journeys to Palermo to "keep an eye on" the lawsuits at the Court of Appeal, he had no personal acquaintance with any of these nobles and entertained an abstract and one-dimensional idea of them, like the public's image of Harlequin or Captain Fracasse.* Prince A. was a spendthrift, Prince B. a woman- izer, the Duke of C. was known for his violence and Baron D. for his gambling, Don Giuseppe E. was quarrelsome, the Marquis F. was an "aesthetic" (he meant "aesthete", which was in turn a euphemism for more reprehensible inclinations), and so forth: each a cut-out cardboard figure unworthy of anyone's respect. Don Batassano's opinions had a strong tendency to be wrong: indeed, it might be said that not a single epithet was correctly applied to a name – or, at the very least, there wasn't a fault that was not fantasti- cally exaggerated, while the actual flaws of character to be found in these personages were entirely unknown to him. His mind was content to work with abstract ideas and drew satisfaction from the thought that the purity of the Ibbas stood out even more clearly against the background of the ancient nobility's corrupt ways.

Ferrara was more familiar with how things stood, but his knowledge too was far from perfect, so that when he tried to refute Don Batassano's more extravagant assertions he lacked the circumstantial evidence to back up his arguments.

And his attempts at defence aroused such moralistic ire in his interlocutor that he soon abandoned them. Besides, the dinner was almost over.

In Ferrara's opinion, it had been excellent. In culinary matters, Donna Laura never strayed far from the beaten track: the food served in her house was Sicilian cooking taken to the utmost degree, with a profusion of dishes and quantity of condiments which made it little less than lethal. The maccheroni literally swam in their oily sauce and were buried beneath a mountain of caciocavallo cheese, the meats were stuffed with fiery salami, and into the puddings, "just rustled up in a hurry", a threefold quantity of the doses of alchermes,* sugar and candied pumpkin prescribed in the recipe was poured. Yet all this seemed delicious to Ferrara – the pinnacle of culinary art. On the rare occasions he had dined with the Salina family, the insipid food he had been served had always disappointed him. Once he was back in Palermo on the following day, however, after handing over the payment of seventy-eight thousand two hundred lire to Prince Fabrizietto,* whose fondness for such dishes as the *coulis de volaille* at the Pré Catelan or Prunier's *timbales d'écrevisses** was well known to him, he described the dishes he had enjoyed at the Ibba home as culinary monstrosities – much to the satisfaction of Salina, who later, during a round of poker at the Club,* passed on Ferrara's account of his visit to his friends, always avid for any news about the legendary Ibba family, provoking much merriment until the stone-faced Peppino San Carlo declared he was holding a full house of queens.

As mentioned just now, there was an intense curiosity about the Ibbas among the aristocratic families of Palermo and their social circle. Since curiosity is the mother of legend, a hundred fantastic stories were spun in those years about their sudden wealth. This was not only due to the puerile, effervescent imaginations of the upper classes, but also to an unconscious sense of unease at seeing how far it was possible, at the beginning of the twentieth century, to amass a vast fortune solely from landed property – a form of wealth which was, as each of these gentlemen knew bitterly from their own experience, more prone to demolition than suited to the construction of fine edifices. These same landowners regarded Ibba's reincarnation of the vast grain fields of the Chiaromonte or Ventimiglia estates in bygone centuries as unreasonable, and sensed that it posed a threat to them. They harboured a veiled hostility to it, not simply because the imposing edifice had been built in large part from material that had once belonged to them, but also because they saw in it – in common with many others, who were at the same time incapable of following a different path or refusing to collaborate – a manifestation of that state of permanent anachronism that prevents Sicily from ever moving forward.

Yet it should be stressed that this sense of unease remained latent, at the level of their collective unconscious, surfacing only in the form of tall stories and humorous anecdotes, as one would expect from a class not well known for its appetite for general ideas. These tall stories, in their primary, most basic form, consisted of exaggerated numbers, which people here always love to distort. Although it would have been easy to check the actual figures, Baldassare Ibba's fortune was estimated as being in the region of hundreds of millions of lire. One person was bold enough to assert that it was worth "almost a billion" – but was quickly shouted down, since back in 1901 such a figure, quite unremarkable today, was so rarely used that hardly anyone knew exactly what it meant: in those days when the value of the lira was pegged to gold reserves, a billion lire was so unreal a sum it was tantamount to nothing. Similar fantasies were woven round the origins of this untold wealth. It was difficult to exaggerate Don Batassano's low-born beginnings (old Corrado Finale, whose mother had been a Santapau, had implied – rather than explicitly asserted – that Ibba was the son of a brother-in-law of his who had lived in Gibilmonte for a time, but almost no one believed him, since it was well known that Finale was in the habit of attributing the real paternity of any passing celebrity – a victorious army general, say, or an acclaimed prima donna – to either himself or one of his relatives). The modest corpse that had caused problems for Don Gaspare, however, was multiplied by ten and then by a hundred, until there was hardly an individual who'd been disposed of in the previous thirty years on the island

(and there were many) whose murder was not ascribed to the Ibbas – for whom, after all, the official records were whiter than white. Perhaps surprisingly, this was the most positive part of the legend, since unpunished acts of physical violence in those days attracted praise. After all, the haloes of Sicilian saints drip with blood.

Further stories had been grafted onto a stock of older inventions: for example, the anecdote told a century earlier about Testasecca, who had had a narrow channel dug on his land and then assembled, at one end of it, the hundreds of cows and thousands of goats he owned and had them all milked at the same time, so that Ferdinand IV, seated at the other end, was treated to the spectacle of a stream of warm, foamy milk running past him. This fable, with its touching air of pastoral poetry that should have given its Theocritean origins away, was now applied to Don Batassano, merely replacing Ferdinand with Umberto I* – and although it was very easy to demonstrate that this latter monarch had never set foot on any part of the Ibba estates, it managed to survive unchallenged.

It was this combination of rancour and fear that, once the game of poker had been concluded, led the conversation back to the subject of the Ibba family. About a dozen of the Club's members, for the most part elderly, were seated on the terrace overlooking a peaceful courtyard under the shade of a tall tree which sent lilac petals down on the assembled group. Waiters in red-and-blue uniforms served ice creams and drinks. From the depths of a wicker armchair the tones of Santa Giulia's voice, angry as always, rose up: "For God's sake, doesn't anyone know exactly how much land this wretched Ibba owns?"

"It *is* known" San Carlo replied, coldly. "Fourteen thousand three hundred and twenty-five hectares."

"That's all? I thought it was more."

"Fourteen thousand my arse! According to people who've actually been there, there can't be less than twenty thousand hectares, as sure as I'm talking to you, and all of it top-quality arable land."

General Lascari, who appeared to be immersed in his reading of *La Tribuna*,* brusquely lowered the newspaper, revealing a splenetic face, lined with fine yellow wrinkles, in which his very white eyeballs stood out, hard and slightly sinister, like the eyes of certain Greek bronzes: "They are twenty-eight thousand, not a jot more or less. My nephew told me. He's a cousin of his administrator's wife. That's the true figure – and there's no point going on about it any more."

Pippo Follonica, a guest from Rome on a short visit to Palermo, gave a laugh. "But really, if you find the subject so interesting, why not send someone to the Land Registry? It's easy to find out the truth – at least this piece of the truth."

Follonica's reasonable suggestion was received without enthusiasm. He had not realized the discussion was driven by passion rather than statistics: their envies, resentments and fears were being batted back and forth among them, and they wouldn't be put to rest by merely consulting a certificate in the Land Registry.

The general became furious. "If I say something, you don't need to check any land or sea registries." Then he recalled the courtesy due to Follonica as a guest, and his tone softened. "My dear Prince, you have no idea what the Land Registry is like here! The registrations are never kept up to date, and you still find the names of owners who sold up and can now be found in the poorhouse."

Faced with such a meticulously argued denial, Follonica changed tactics. "All right, let's admit then that we don't know how many acres he owns – but at least we can find out just how much this yokel who seems to obsess you is worth!"

"Of course. Eight million, all told."

"My arse!" – that was Santa Giulia's trademark opening – "My arse! Not a cent less than twelve million!"

"Do any of you live in the real world? None of you knows the slightest thing! He's worth twenty-five million in land alone. Then there are the rents, the capital sums he's loaned and not yet transformed into property, the value of the livestock... At least another fifteen million." The general had now laid his newspaper down and was moving about irritably in his chair. His peremptory tone had always annoyed the other members of the Club: each of them wished to be the only one who could make incontrovertible remarks. In their newly awakened pique, they quickly formed an alliance against him and, abandoning all regard for the truth of the matter, sent the value of Ibba's patrimony into free fall. "Stuff and nonsense. With saints and money, cut the baloney. If Baldassare Ibba has ten million, everything included, that's being generous." The figure had been plucked out of nowhere, merely to support the argument, but since it was what everyone wanted, it calmed the waters, except for the general who, faced with the arrayed strength of his nine adversaries, made helpless gestures from his chair.

A waiter entered carrying a long wooden stick with a wad of cloth on the end dipped in alcohol and set aflame. The soft rays of the setting sun were replaced by the rigid beams of the gas chandelier. The Roman guest was very amused: it was his first visit to Sicily and, over the five days he had spent in Palermo, he had been received in many houses and had started to change his mind about the reputation of the city's inhabitants for provincialism: he had found the dinners served correctly, the salons elegant and the women gracious. But now this impassioned discussion about the wealth of an individual whom none of the contenders in the argument either knew or wished to know, the brazen exaggerations and forceful but pointless gesticulating were making him return to his former opinions: the scene reminded him of nothing so much as the conversations he heard in Fondi or Palestrina* when he had to go and check up on his estates there, or even the episodes in *Tartarin* set in Bézuquet's pharmacy,* of which he'd kept a fond memory ever since he'd first read the book. He would have plenty of stories to tell his friends when he returned to Rome in a week's time. But he was mistaken: he was too much a man of the world to extend his observations beyond the most superficial of appearances – and what he took for a comic display of provincial manners was no such thing: it was the tragic contortions of a landowning class that saw its former superiority on the wane – and with it their reason for existing and their social continuity – and that as a result sought, in their histrionic exaggerations and spurious disparagements, an outlet for their rage and a relief for their fears.

Since it was impossible to ascertain the truth of the matter, the conversation moved on to other topics – still on the subject of Baldassare Ibba and his private affairs, but now focused on his personal life.

"He lives like a monk. He gets up at four in the morning and goes to the town square to hire the day labourers. He spends the whole day on administration, eats only pasta and vegetables with a bit of oil, and goes to bed at eight o'clock."

Salina protested: "A monk with a wife and eight children? Come on. One of my employees spent a day with him recently. The house is nothing to look at, but it's large and comfortable – a decent place in short. His wife must have been pretty in her day, and the children are well dressed – actually one of them is doing his studies here in Palermo. And as I told you before, their cooking is heavy, but there's certainly no shortage of it."

But the general wouldn't give way. "The trouble with you, Salina, is that you believe everything you're told – or rather your employee, who must be a perfect idiot, has been fooled by them. Bread, cheese and an oil lamp to light him to bed – that's how Ibba spends his days, that's how he really lives. Obviously, when someone from Palermo comes to visit, he puts on a show to impress him – or that he thinks will impress him."

Santa Giulia urgently wanted to impart some information, and twisted and turned in his chair: he beat his elegantly shod feet on the floor, his hands were shaking, and ash from his cigarette fell like snow on his suit. "Gentlemen, gentlemen, it's clear you don't know a damn thing – you're all completely wrong. I'm the only one who knows what the real situation is. The wife of one of my wardens comes from Torrebella, a stone's throw from Gibilmonte. She goes every now and then to visit her married sister who lives there, and gets all the news from her. You can't get a more reliable source than that, can you?" He searched the faces of the others for confirmation of this and, since they all looked amused, he thought they concurred. Although there was no bashful ear around, he lowered his voice: without this melodramatic gesture, his revelations would have had less of an effect. "Four kilometres outside Gibilmonte, Don Baldassare has had a mansion built for himself, with all the finest luxuries – furniture from Salci and suchlike." Remembered extracts from the pages of Catulle Mendès's novels,* nostalgic reminiscences of Parisian

brothels, long-nurtured but never fulfilled desires – all found
their way into Santa Giulia's fantasies. "He got Rochegrosse,*
the famous painter, to come from Paris to paint the rooms
with frescoes. He stayed three months in Gibilmonte and
charged a hundred thousand lire a month." (It was true
that Rochegrosse had visited Sicily two years before: he had
stayed a week with his wife and three children, and returned
home after an uneventful tour including the Palatine Chapel,
the temple of Segesta and the Latomia in Siracusa.) "It cost
him a fortune! But what frescoes! They could revive a dead
man. Naked women – all naked – dancing and drinking and
having intercourse with men and with each other in all the
positions and ways you can think of. They're masterpieces!
All the pleasures – like an encyclopedia – yes, an encyclopedia of pleasure! Of course, give a Parisian a hundred
thousand lire a month and that's what you'd expect... Ibba
receives dozens of women there – Italians, French, German,
Spanish. I know for a fact that Otero* has been there too.
Yes, Batassano has built his own 'Parc-aux-Cerfs' down
there, like Louis XVI's."*

This time Santa Giulia had made a big impression: the
others were listening to him agape. Not because they
believed any of it, but because they were captivated by
the sheer poetry of the fantasy. Each of them would have
liked to have Ibba's millions just so they could spin such
resplendent moonshine. The first to shake himself free of
the spell was the general.

"And how come you know about all this? You've been to the house? Were you one of the odalisques or one of the eunuchs?"

They all laughed, including Santa Giulia.

"I've already told you. The wife of my warden, Antonio, saw those paintings."

"Bravo! Then your warden's a cuckold!"

"Cuckold my arse! She went there to take some sheets she'd washed. She wasn't allowed in, but a window was open and she saw everything."

The extreme fragility of this castle of lies was obvious to all, but it was so beautiful – women's thighs, nameless obscenities, celebrated painters and hundred-grand bank-notes – that no one had any wish to blow on it and bring it tumbling down.

Salina pulled out his watch. "Good Lord! It's eight o'clock already! I must go home and dress. They're doing *La traviata* at the Politeama with Bellincioni this evening – and the way she sings 'Amami, Alfredo!'* is just unmissable. I'll see you all in the private box."

Notes

p. 3, *Henry Brulard*: Written in 1835–36 and published posthumously, *Vie de Henry Brulard* (*Life of Henry Brulard*) is an autobiographical work by Stendhal (1783–1842).

p. 4, *aux petits soins*: "Making a fuss over me" (French).

p. 5, *when I was just a few days older than three and a half*: The early scenes of the 'Memories' take place at the Palazzo Lampedusa in Via Lampedusa, Palermo. The palazzo, dating back to the late sixteenth century, originally belonged to the Aragon family, who set up a school for girls there in around 1630. A few decades later, it fell in a state of disrepair. It was acquired and restored in the 1750s by Ferdinando II Maria (1697–1775), 4th Prince of Lampedusa, 5th Duke of Palma, an important public figure of his time and perhaps the most prominent member of the Lampedusa family. It will be the residence of the Lampedusas until 1943, when the palazzo was destroyed by the Allied bombings.

p. 6, *my mother*: Beatrice Mastrogiovanni Tasca di Cutò (1870–1946).

p. 7, *Bon Signour*: "Good Lord" (Piedmontese dialect).

p. 7, *My father*: Giulio Tomasi (1868–1934), 10th Prince of Lampedusa and 11th Duke of Palma.

p. 7, *King Umberto had been assassinated at Monza*: King Umberto I of Italy (1844–1900), who had already survived two previous assassination attempts in 1878 and 1897, was killed by the anarchist Gaetano Bresci (1869–1901) in Monza on 29th July 1900.

p. 8, *Messina earthquake (28th December 1908)*: One of the greatest natural disasters in recent history: some 200,000 people are estimated to have been killed. Giuseppe's aunt Lina (Nicoletta, 1872–1908) Cianciafara (the mother of Filippo in the following paragraph, who later became a photographer) and her husband were among the victims.

p. 8, *my grandfather's*: Lampedusa's paternal grandfather, Giuseppe Tomasi (1838–1908), 9th Prince of Lampedusa and 10th Duke of Palma.

p. 8, *my grandmother's*: Lampedusa's paternal grandmother, Stefania Papè e Vanni (1840–1913).

p. 8, *my grandfather had already been dead for just over a year*: He had actually died on 19th October 1908.

p. 8, *Piccolo cousins*: Agata Giovanna (1891–1974), Casimiro (1894–1970) and Lucio (1901–69) Piccolo. In 1908 they lived in an art-deco villa on Via della Libertà near Piazza delle Croci. In the late Twenties, they nearly went bankrupt after a failed building-development project on the grounds of the villa. In 1933 they moved to their country house at Capo d'Orlando, around 140 km from Palermo, with their mother Teresa (1871–1952), sister of Lampedusa's mother Beatrice.

p. 9, *dreadnoughts*: A heavily armed battleship that was common in the early twentieth century. Lampedusa uses the English word in the text.

p. 10, *Grazzie, ragazzo*: "Thank you, lad" (Emilian dialect). People from the Emilia region (roughly the west and north-west parts of the Emilia-Romagna district) tend to pronounce the Zs like Ss, as Lampedusa is trying to indicate with his spelling.

p. 10, *accident, murder and suicide*: Three years after the death of Lina, Giuseppe's aunt Giulia Trigona di Sant'Elia (see first note to p. 64) was murdered in Rome by her lover, Vincenzo Paternò del Cugno. His other aunt Maria (1877–1923) never married and ended up committing suicide.

p. 10, *the Florio family… Favignana*: The Florios were one of the richest and most prominent families of Palermo at that time. Favignana is an island off the west coast of Sicily between Trapani and Marsala.

p. 11, *Signora Florio (the "godlike beauty" Franca)*: Franca Florio (1873–1950) was one of the most celebrated beauties of the *belle époque*. She was married to Ignazio Florio (1869–1957), a great industrialist and banker.

p. 11, *Eugénie, the former Empress of France*: Eugénie de Montijo (1826–1920), wife of Napoleon III (1808–73) and Empress Consort of France from 1853 to 1871.

p. 11, *Quel joli petit*: "What a lovely child" (French).

p. 13, *our house*: The Palazzo Lampedusa in Palermo.

p. 15, *Monte Pellegrino... Monreale*: Monte Pellegrino is a promontory facing east on the Bay of Palermo. Porta Nuova is the main entryway to Palermo from the hill town of Monreale, situated south-west of the city.

p. 16, *catodi*: An Italianized form of the Sicilian word *catoiu* (from the Greek κατώγειον), which denotes slum-like dwellings.

p. 17, *fine grey Billiemi stone*: A high-quality marble from the quarries of Mount Billiemi near Palermo. The quarries belonged to the Tomasi family, as part of the barony of Torretta.

p. 17, *tocchetto*: A local term denoting a loggia leading to the first-floor apartments, as explained later on p. 19.

p. 19, *Dis à Moffo qu'il est un mufle*: "Tell Moffo he is a boor" (French).

p. 20, *lambris*: Marble or wood panelling decorating the lower part of a wall.

p. 21, *those from Mount Sinai*: Presumably the reference is to the rays of light beaming from Moses's face when he descended from Mount Sinai after talking to God (Exodus 34:29–35).

p. 21, *wicked joke*: In English in the text.

p. 22, *day nursery*: In English in the text.

p. 23, *Santa Margherita di Belice... visited those*: Santa Margherita di Belice, a town in the province of Agrigento, around 70 km south-west of Palermo; Bagheria, a town around 15 km east of Palermo; Torretta, a town around 20 km west of Palermo; Raitano, a locality situated in the Piana dei Colli, a valley on the northern border of Palermo; Palma di Montechiaro, a town in the province of Agrigento, around 150 km south of Palermo. Palma was founded by Lampedusa's ancestors, Carlo (1614–75) and Giulio (1614–69) Tomasi e Caro, in 1637.

p. 23, *Ferdinand IV... as Murat ruled over Naples*: King Ferdinand IV of Naples (1751–1825) and his consort Maria Carolina of Austria (1752–1814) lived in exile during Joachim Murat's (1767–1815) rule of Naples between 1808 and 1815. This was the second time the King had been exiled to Sicily. The Prince Cutò mentioned in the text is Alessandro III Filangeri, 6th Prince of Cutò and Viceroy (*Luogotenente*) of Sicily between 1803 and 1806. He redecorated the palazzo in order to host the royal couple. It was rumoured that his son Niccolò (Niccolò I, 7th Prince of Cutò, 1760–1839) was the Queen Consort's lover.

p. 23, *my grandmother Cutò*: Giovanna Filangeri Clerici (1850–91), 9th Princess of Cutò. She had married Lucio Mastrogiovanni Tasca d'Almerita (1842–1918) in 1867.

p. 23, *up to date*: In English in the text.

p. 24, *comfort*: In English in the text.

p. 24, *électrique*: "Electric car" (French).

p. 24, *Anna I*: I.e. Anna the First – a first nursemaid by the name of Anna, who will be later replaced by another Anna (Anna II, see p. 45).

p. 24, *our accountant Ferrara*: See first note to p. 131.

p. 25, *Carini… landed*: Carini, Cinisi and Partinico are towns west of Palermo. Lo Zucco is a large landed estate situated between Cinisi and Partinico. The Expedition of the Thousand, led by Giuseppe Garibaldi (1807–82), landed at Marsala, a city at the westernmost point of Sicily, on 11th May 1860.

p. 25, *Castelvetrano*: A town in the province of Trapani, around 100 km south-west of Palermo.

p. 26, *Partanna*: A town in the province of Trapani, around 10 km north-west of Castelvetrano.

p. 26, *brigadiere*: A Carabinieri officer whose rank is equivalent to that of staff sergeant in the army.

p. 26, *like Fattori's light cavalrymen*: Giovanni Fattori (1825–1908) was the author of a number of celebrated paintings depicting light cavalrymen and other military subjects.

p. 27, *A Spanish woman knows how to love*: A line from the famous 1906 song 'La Spagnola' ('The Spanish Woman') by Vincenzo di Chiara (1864–1937).

p. 28, *Venaria, the hunting lodge which belonged to us*: The hunting lodge had been built by Alessandro II Filangeri (1696–1761), 4th Prince of Cutò. It was reduced to ruins by the 1968 Belice earthquake.

p. 29, *Nofrio*: Short for Onofrio.

p. 29, *The House*: The title is not in Lampedusa's hand.

p. 30, *a cross adorned with nine bells*: The escutcheon of the coat of arms of the Filangeri di Cutò family.

p. 30, *Ferdinand II's gentleman of the royal bedchamber*: Alessandro IV Filangeri, 8th Prince of Cutò (see first note to p. 53), gentleman of the bedchamber of King Ferdinand II of the Two Sicilies (1810–59) and father of Giovanna Filangeri di Cutò, Lampedusa's maternal grandmother (see third to note to p. 23).

p. 30, *Riccardo... the Gallic hordes in 1796*: Riccardo (or Richard) Filangeri (*c.*1195–1254/63) played an important role during the Sixth Crusade (1228–29) as the right-hand man of King Frederick II (1194–1250) and remained in the Holy Land until 1242. Of Raimondo and the other Riccardo not much is known other than what is reported here by Lampedusa, who is quoting from memory the labels beneath the paintings. The Sicilian Vespers were a 1282 uprising against French rule, leading to a long war on the island. Riccardo, who was living in exile at the Court of Aragon since 1266, may have been sent on purpose to Sicily to initiate the rebellion. For Niccolò I, see second note to p. 23.

p. 31, *Angerius*: Angerius (d.1104) was a knight in the retinue of Robert Guiscard (*c.*1015–85), one of the leading figures in the Norman conquest of southern Italy and Sicily. He was the founder of the Filangeri family, whose name derives from the Latin *filii Angerii* (sons of

Angerius). One of Angerius's sons, Tancredi, is listed among the Norman barons present at the 1130 coronation in Palermo of Roger II of Sicily (1095–1154).

p. 31, *stile di badia*: "Abbey style" (Italian).

p. 32, *Almost all the works… from the author*: The *Encyclopédie*, published between 1751 and 1772 and edited by Denis Diderot (1713–84) and Jean-Baptiste le Rond d'Alembert (1717–83) is the landmark work of the French Enlightenment. Voltaire is the pseudonym of the French philosopher and polymath François-Marie Arouet (1694–1778) – the *editio princeps* of his works, edited by Pierre Beaumarchais (1732–99), is the seventy-volume edition printed in Kehl between 1787 and 1791. The fortress of Kehl was rented for twenty years from the Margrave of Baden-Baden for the purpose. Bernard Le Bovier de Fontenelle (1657–1757) was a French writer. Claude Adrien Helvétius (1715–71) was a French author and man of letters. Niccolò is the above-mentioned Niccolò Filangeri (see second note to p. 23). Jean de La Fontaine (1621–95) was the celebrated author of the *Fables* (1668–94). The *History of Napoleon* was an early biography of the French ruler by Jacques Marquet de Montbreton, Baron of Norvins (1769–1854), with illustrations by Auguste Raffet (1804–60) and Horace Vernet (1789–1863). Émile Zola (1840–1902) was the author, among other things, of a twenty-volume cycle of naturalist novels, the *Rougon-Macquart* (1871–93), which had a great influence on many other writers across

Europe, including the Sicilian-born novelist Giuseppe Verga (1840–1922), founder of the Verismo realist school and author of I Malavoglia (The Malavoglias or The House by the Medlar Tree, 1881). The word "mellow" is in English in the text.

p. 32, *ouistitis*: "Marmosets" (French).

p. 33, *"King Big Nose" himself*: Ferdinand I of the Two Sicilies (1751–1825).

p. 33, *succhi d'erba*: Painted imitations of tapestries.

p. 33, *Gerusalemme Liberata*: The poetical masterpiece of Torquato Tasso (1544–95).

p. 33, *House of the Metzengerstein*: A reference to 'Metzengerstein', a short story by Edgar Allan Poe (1809–49). In misquoting the title (in English in the text), Lampedusa may have also been thinking of Poe's 'The Fall of the House of Usher'.

p. 33, *This particular succo d'erba still belongs to me*: Lampedusa's memory failed him in this case: the *succo d'erba* he owned represented Esther preparing herself to meet King Ahasuerus.

p. 34, *fall of Port Arthur*: The fall of Port Arthur – the Russians' surrender of their naval base in Manchuria to the Japanese – took place on 2nd January 1905.

p. 34, *scopone*: A card game.

p. 35, *Politeama... fast*: I.e. dissipated (in English in the text). For the Politeama, see note to p. 152.

p. 35, *Franz Joseph*: Franz Joseph I of Austria (1830–1916).

p. 37, *'A Signura raccumanna: 'u cascavaddu*: "The Lady recommends: caciocavallo cheese (to be grated on the maccheroni pasta)" (Sicilian dialect).

p. 40, *Pietro Scalea*: The politician Pietro Lanza di Scalea (1863–1938).

p. 42, *Salon*: An art exhibition organized by the Académie des Beaux-Arts in Paris.

p. 42, *that mighty hunter before the Lord*: Lampedusa's grandfather is jocularly associated with Nimrod, who in Genesis 10:9 is described in the same terms. Lampedusa may have also been thinking of Dante's description of Nimrod in the *Inferno* – a giant and a "bewildered soul" (*Inferno* XXXI, 74).

p. 43, *my cynegetic career*: I.e. my career as a hunter.

p. 43, *campieri*: Estate guards, wardens.

p. 43, *l'épée… de l'Empire*: "The sword of the brave General Count Delort reddened with the blood of the enemies of the Empire" (French).

p. 44, *vernis Martin*: A type of imitation lacquer.

p. 45, *bains de son*: "Bran baths" (French).

p. 45, *Piccolo cousins at Capo d'Orlando*: See third note to p. 8.

p. 46, *Olivella church in Palermo*: The Chiesa di Sant'Ignazio all'Olivella.

p. 46, *plaque tournante*: "Hub" (French).

p. 47, *a double-headed eagle with a bell-adorned cross on its breast*: The coat of arms of the Filangeri di Cutò family.

p. 47, *Riccardo Filangeri engaged in the defence of Antioch*: See third note to p. 30.

p. 47, *Grousset*: René Grousset (1885–1952), author of a famous *Histoire des croisades* (1934–36).

p. 48, *Lady of the Camellias*: The heroine of the eponymous 1848 novel by Alexandre Dumas, *fils*, subsequently adapted for the stage.

p. 48, *vert Nil*: "Nile-green" (French).

p. 49, *Scribe... Torelli*: The playwrights Eugène Scribe (1791–1861), Gerolamo Rovetta (1851–1910), Victorien Sardou (1831–1908), Paolo Giacometti (1816–82) and Achille Torelli (1841–1922).

p. 49, *pochade*: "Sketch" (French).

p. 49, *garden party*: In English in the text.

p. 50, *Duse*: Eleonora Duse (1858–1924).

p. 50, *office*: In English in the text.

p. 50, *Prince Alessandro*: Alessandro III Filangeri, 6th Prince of Cutò (see second note to p. 23).

p. 51, *collier de chien*: "Neckband" (French).

p. 52, *Neptune... Amphitrite*: In Roman mythology, Neptune was the god of the sea – the equivalent of Poseidon for the Greeks. The sea goddess Amphitrite was Poseidon's wife, while Neptune's consort was in fact Salacia.

p. 52, *toilette*: "Outfit" (French).

p. 53, *great-grandfather... Marina*: Lampedusa's great-grandfather was Alessandro IV Filangeri (1802–54), 8th Prince of Cutò. It is not clear what misdemeanours he may have committed on the Marina (another name for the Foro Italico, the seafront promenade in front of the Palazzo Lanza Tomasi, a well-known meeting point for lovers), but the first translator of 'Childhood Memories', Archibald Colquhon (1913–64), in his note to the passage, reports that Alessandro's misdeameanour had been to drive in his carriage down the Marina completely naked – a piece of information he may have collected during his stay in Palermo in July 1962 for the filming of *The Leopard*. Alessandro had a bad reputation, especially as a womanizer. After divorcing from his first wife, he married the famous soprano Teresa Merli Clerici (1816–97) in 1850.

p. 53, *coming back… throw it away*: This passage, struck out in the text, has been reused in Part One of *The Leopard*, where Don Onofrio is said to have ensured that a shot glass of liqueur left half full by the Princess before leaving Donnafugata is still found in the same place a year later, its content evaporated and reduced to sugar. This suggests that 'Childhood Memories' may have been written at the same time as Part Two of *The Leopard*, thus forming its emotional background.

p. 54, *boîte à musique*: "Music box" (French).

p. 55, *pains à cacheter*: Wafer used for sealing letters (French).

p. 55, *Doré's illustrations to scenes from Ariosto*: A reference to Gustave Doré's (1832–83) famous engravings of Ludovico Ariosto's (1474–1533) *Orlando Furioso*.

p. 56, *Dis*: The City of Dis, the lower part of Dante's Inferno.

p. 56, *Dance, and Provençal song, and sunburnt mirth*: Line 14 of John Keats's (1795–1821) 'Ode to a Nightingale'. In English in the text.

p. 56, *mirth*: In English in the text.

p. 56, *stornelli*: Short songs, usually improvised.

p. 57, *'na camurrìa*: Literally, a venereal disease, but figuratively a blight, an annoying thing (Sicilian dialect).

p. 57, *lotus-eaters*: In English in the text.

p. 57, *cannæ*: Canna lilies (Latin).

p. 58, *Carducci's 'Hymn to Satan'… reason*: Lines 193–96 of Giosuè Carducci's (1835–1907) 'Hymn to Satan' (written 1863, published 1865).

p. 58, *I excommunicate you… Mastai*: Lines 168 and 170 (slightly misquoted) of Giosuè Carducci's 1868 poem 'Per Eduardo Corazzini', from Book One of his *Giambi ed epodi* (1867–69), a collection of often polemical verses. His target, in this and other works, is Pope Pius IX (born Giovanni Maria Mastai Ferretti, 1792–1878), called ironically and spitefully "Citizen Mastai" in the last line of his poem 'The Song of Love' (written 1877, published 1878).

p. 59, *dog cart*: Here and in the following paragraph, in English.

p. 60, *double row of cypress trees… San Guido*: Lampedusa is here referring to another famous poem by Giosuè

Carducci, 'Davanti San Guido' (1874). The first two lines read: 'The cypress trees that, at Bolgheri, tall and lean / Go from San Guido in a double row.'

p. 61, *timballi di maccheroni alla Talleyrand*: A Sicilian dish: timbales of pasta.

p. 64, *my aunt Giulia Trigona*: Giulia Trigona di Sant'Elia (1876–1911), a lady-in-waiting to Elena (1873–1952), Queen Consort of Italy, who had married Romualdo Trigona di Sant'Elia (1870–1929) in 1895.

p. 64, *Giovanna… Romualdo*: Giulia's second daughter and husband, respectively.

p. 65, *Xaxa*: Pronounced "Sciascia" in Sicilian.

p. 65, *mero et mixto system*: Whereby all political, administrative, fiscal and judiciary powers are delegated to a feudatory.

p. 66, *boîtes*: Nightclubs (French).

p. 66, *Ville Lumière*: The City of Lights, i.e. Paris.

p. 66, *le grand escogriffe*: "The tall beanpole" (French).

p. 67, *Guide*: A regiment of troopers.

p. 67, *Custoza*: Despite its considerable numerical advantage, the Italian army was defeated by the Austrian Imperial army at the Battle of Custoza on 24th June 1866 during the Third Italian War of Independence.

p. 68, *Salgari's adventure novel The Caribbean Queen… Black Corsair and Carmaux's braggadocio*: Emilio Salgari (1862–1911) was a prolific author of young-adult fiction, including a cycle of five novels, "The

Corsairs of the Antilles" (1898–1908), the most famous volume of which was *The Black Corsair*, published in 1898 and followed three years later by *The Queen of the Caribbeans*.

p. 68, *Pestalozzi and James*: The Swiss pedagogue Johann Heinrich Pestalozzi (1746–1827) and the American philosopher and educator William James (1842–1910), brother of the novelist Henry James (1843–1916).

p. 68, *spell words with double consonants and accented syllables*: The two main problem areas for Italian children learning to spell.

p. 69, *two Bs*: A "wicked joke" directed at Lampedusa's uncle, Senator Pietro Tomasi della Torretta (1873–1962). Sicilians tend, at times, to stress the pronunciation of consonants so that they sound like double consonants and, at other times, unstress double consonants so that they sound like single consonants. Lampedusa is hinting that Torretta would have been surprised – unlike himself, who had been educated by Donna Carmela – to see so many misspellings of the word "*Repubblica*", as he would have expected it to be written "*Reppublica*". The joke was struck out in Lampedusa's notebook – perhaps by his wife Licy.

p. 69, *le chien, le chat, le cheval*: "The dog, the cat, the horse" (French).

p. 70, *quartare*: "Pitchers" (Sicilian dialect).

p. 71, *cantari*: "Chamberpots" (Sicilian dialect).

p. 75, *a three-syllable word... misfortunes*: The three-syllable word would have been *"cornuto"* ("cuckold"), a common generic insult in Sicily.

p. 78, *heavy with ominous signs*: A parody of Fascist bombastic Latinate propaganda language. The Italian reads: *"onusto di presagi"*. A similar expression, *"onusto di cattivi presagi"* ("ominously unlucky"), was used by Lampedusa in his 'Childhood Memories' (see p. 15).

p. 81, *Girì*: Short for Girolamo.

p. 81, *Standa*: The name of a department store.

p. 85, *The Siren*: This translation is based on the typescript provided by Lampedusa's widow in 1961 (see Note on the Texts). A manuscript fragment, in Lampedusa's own hand, from an earlier version of 'The Siren' has survived. Given the paucity of autograph manuscripts of Lampedusa's writings, this in itself makes the fragment remarkable but, as a preliminary version of a text we have in finished form (the text as translated in this edition) and despite its brevity – we have only the pages for the section of the story immediately after the encounter with Ligeia to the coming of the storm when she departs – it affords a unique and fascinating insight into the way Lampedusa worked on his writing. The immediate impression is of greater elaboration, a more ornate patterning of the prose surface in the finished text as compared to the early draft. There are also significant differences in the later version in terms of content and characterization.

p. 85, *tota*: "Girlfriend" (Piedmontese dialect).

p. 85, *causa mali tanti*: "The cause of such grief" (Latin).

p. 85, *porcoun*: "Pig" (Piedmontese dialect).

p. 86, *Monsù... Cerea monsù*: "Sir... All the best, Sir" (Piedmontese dialect).

p. 87, *On my right*: The text says again "On my left", but it is probably a dictation mistake (see Note on the Texts).

p. 88, *MinCulPop*: And abbreviated form of Ministero della Cultura Popolare (Ministry of Popular Culture), a Fascist government department overlooking all forms of popular culture and Party propaganda.

p. 89, *Chiel... Chiel l'è 'l senatour Rosario La Ciura*: "That man?... That man is Senator Rosario La Ciura" (Piedmontese dialect).

p. 90, *Lincean Academy*: Accademia dei Lincei in Italian, one of the most ancient and prestigious academies in Italy, founded in 1603 and the first one devoted to science.

p. 90, *Teubner*: A German publisher that has brought out many "definitive" editions of classical works.

p. 90, *Accademia d'Italia*: A cultural academy founded by the Fascist government in 1926 and dissolved at the end of the war. Its members included leading scholars and cultural figures who had pledged their allegiance to the regime.

p. 91, *Mr Gillette*: King C. Gillette (1855–1932), entrepreneur and inventor of the safety razor.

p. 92, *Corbera*: The same family name as the protagonist of *The Leopard*, Fabrizio Corbera, Prince of Salina. The Corberas were an ancient Catalan family who had been in the service of the Aragon royals since the time of the Sicilian Vespers (see third note to p. 30). The Corberas owned the Barony of Misilindino, in the Belice valley, since the 1450s. Because of debt they were later dispossessed, and the barony was reacquired in 1625 by Elisabetta Corbera, who had married Francesco Filangeri, before being broken up in 1668 following a lawsuit from the dispossessed Corberas. The Filangeris expanded their domains in the area through a series of advantageous marriages, and at the time of Alessandro II Filangeri (see note to p. 28) took up the palazzo in Santa Margherita as their main seat.

p. 94, *all the various stratagems a Leopard uses to adapt*: This phrase renders Lampedusa's "*Gattoparderie*", a word that has entered the Italian vocabulary after the publication of *The Leopard*.

p. 95, *Paolo Orsi*: Paolo Orsi (1859–1935) was a famous Italian archaelogist and classicist.

p. 95, *Nebrodi mountains*: A mountain range running along the north-east of Sicily.

p. 95, *Melilli's honey*: Melilli is a town around 20 km northwest of Siracusa, renowned for the production of honey.

p. 95, *Castellammare*: Castellammare del Golfo, a town in the province of Trapani.

p. 96, *rizzi*: "Sea urchins" (Sicilian dialect).

p. 101, *cousette*: Seamstress (French).

p. 101, *L'è monsù Corbera?*: "Is that Mr Corbera?" (Piedmontese dialect).

p. 102, *lokums*: Turkish delights.

p. 103, *the collected plays of Tirso de Molina… the works of H.G. Wells*: A reference to the Spanish dramatist Tirso de Molina (1579–1648), the German writer Friedrich de la Motte Fouqué (1777–1843) – author of the novella *Undine* (1811), adapted for the stage by the French dramatist Jean Giraudoux (1882–1944) in 1938 – and the science-fiction writer H.G. Wells (1866–1946). In la Motte Fouqué's story, the water spirit Undine marries the knight Huldebrand in order to acquire a soul.

p. 105, *Balilla*: A car produced by Fiat.

p. 106, *A sea-change… Siren tears*: The two quotes, in English in the text, are respectively from Shakespeare's *The Tempest* (Act I, Sc. 2, 565) and from his *Sonnets* (CXIX, 1).

p. 107, *famulus*: "Servant" (Latin).

p. 107, *Nervi or Arenzano*: Two fishing villages along the Ligurian coast.

p. 108, *I had done three months of my military service there*: This passage shows the clear autobiographical element of the story. After training in Messina from towards the end of 1915, Lampedusa was appointed Corporal in May 1916 and assigned to a battery stationed in Augusta. In 1917, Lampedusa trained at the Military Academy in Turin to become an officer, and was sent to the front in September, just a month before the famous Battle of Caporetto (24th October–19th November 1917).

p. 108, *dopolavoristi*: Members of a leisure and recreational organization (the *dopolavoro*) created by the Fascist government in 1925.

p. 109, *Collina*: The collective name of hills on the east side of the city of Turin.

p. 112, *San Berillo*: A historic quarter of Catania, now demolished.

p. 117, *I am Ligeia, Calliope is my mother*: In Greek mythology Ligeia (according to some sources) was one of the sirens. Calliope is the Muse of epic poetry.

p. 118, *Une Passion dans le désert*: An 1830 story by Honoré de Balzac (1799–1850), revised and republished in 1837.

p. 118, *Commendatore… Leporello*: Two characters from Wolfgang Amadeus Mozart's (1756–91) opera *Don Giovanni* (1787), with a libretto by Lorenzo da Ponte (1749–1838).

p. 119, *his right thumb and index finger curled an imaginary moustache at the corner of his mouth*: A gesture of appreciation and congratulation.

p. 122, *Ponte Vecchio*: The famous bridge in Florence over the Arno river.

p. 125, *Marmarica*: A North African region between Egypt and Libya.

p. 130, *Batassano*: A vernacular mispronunciation of the name Baldassare.

p. 131, *the agent for the Prince of Salina, Ferrara*: The current Prince of Salina is Fabrizietto, the grandson of Don Fabrizio, the protagonist of Lampedusa's *The Leopard*, of which *The Blind Kittens* was meant to be a sequel. Ferrara, the bookkeeper, is a descendant of the Ferrara who talks to Don Fabrizio in the first chapter of *The Leopard*. See also 'Childhood Memories', p. 24.

p. 131, *eighty of the large pink notes*: Eighty one-thousand-lire notes.

p. 131, *It was true… working for the Salinas*: In 1866, five years after the unification of the country, the new Italian government issued a controversial law ratifying the expropriation of all ecclesiastical buildings excluding those still used for religious services. This law affected southern Italy especially. A Church Fund ("Fondo per il Culto") was established, which collected the payments of old feudal obligations (mostly to do with the maintenance and lighting of religious buildings). Don Batassano and his notary know that the Salinas have already been exempted from their obligations through a past lump-sum payment, yet Ferrara is unaware of it and takes out an extra 1,600 lire from the value of the property as a deposit against the Church Fund liabilities.

p. 133, *brigadiere*: See second note to p. 26.

p. 134, *Ragionier*: "Accountant" or "Bookkeeper" (Italian), also used at times as a general title of courtesy.

p. 136, *the Thousand landed*: See first note to p. 25.

p. 137, *Napoleon at Austerlitz*: The Battle of Austerlitz (2nd December 1805) was one of Napoleon's greatest victories.

p. 137, *Balate*: The name suggests "dry, rocky terrain" (Sicilian dialect).

p. 138, *Frederick II*: See third note to p. 30.

p. 139, *the old prince Fabrizio*: See first note to p. 131.

p. 139, *History of the Bourbons of Naples by La Cecilia*: A work by Giovanni La Cecilia (1801–80).

p. 139, *he was already twenty years old*: The school-leaving certificate is normally obtained at the age of eighteen.

p. 141, *Harlequin or Captain Fracasse*: Characters of puppet-theatre shows.

p. 142, *alchermes*: An Italian liqueur.

p. 142, *The payment... Prince Fabrizietto*: For Prince Fabrizietto, see the first note to p. 131. It is not clear whether the missing 200 lire from the transaction have been withheld (as an agency fee) or stealthily pocketed by Ferrara. It could, of course, be a mistake by Lampedusa, who was not very strict in matters of money.

p. 142, *coulis de volaille at the Pré Catelan or Prunier's timbales d'écrevisses*: Pré Catelan and Prunier are famous Parisian restaurants. *Coulis de volaille* is a kind of chicken stew, while the *timbales d'écrevisses* are crayfish flans.

p. 142, *the Club*: The aristocratic Circolo Bellini in Palermo.

p. 145, *Its Theocritan origins... Umberto I*: For Ferdinand IV and Umberto I, see second note to p. 23 and third note to p. 7 respectively. The Greek poet Theocritus (fl.3rd century BC) is regarded as the creator of the bucolic genre of poetry.

p. 146, *La Tribuna*: A popular daily which ran from 1883 to 1946.

p. 148, *Fondi or Palestrina*: Two towns, respectively around 120 and 40 km from Rome.

p. 148, *the episodes in Tartarin set in Bézuquet's pharmacy*: A reference to the novel *Tartarin de Tarascon* (1872) by Alphonse Daudet (1840–97).

p. 150, *the pages of Catulle Mendès's novels*: A reference to the French poet and novelist Catulle Mendès (1841–1909).

p. 151, *Rochegrosse*: The French decorative painter Georges Rochegrosse (1859–1938).

p. 151, *Otero*: "La Belle" Otero (1868–1965), a Spanish actress, dancer and courtesan.

p. 151, *his own 'Parc-aux-Cerfs' down there, like Louis XVI's*: It was in fact Louis XV (1710–74) who had built the Parc-aux-Cerfs mansion at Versailles, where he could meet his many mistresses. Lampedusa's mistake is probably intentional.

p. 152, *La traviata... 'Amami, Alfredo'*: Gemma Bellincioni (1864–1950) was a celebrated soprano, famous for her interpretation of Violetta in Giuseppe Verdi's (1813–1901) opera *La traviata* (1853), of which 'Amami, Alfredo!' is one of the most popular passages. The Politeama is the main theatre, opera house and music hall in Palermo. Bellincioni performed in Palermo in 1904, but at the Teatro Massimo, not the Politeama as stated by Lampedusa, who would have been seven at the time.

Biographical Note

Giuseppe Tomasi di Lampedusa was born on 23rd December 1896 in Palermo, Sicily. At the turn of the century, the city was very much caught between the old and the new. On the one hand the wealthy entrepreneurs centring around the Florio family, on the other a handful of ancient, noble families, once at the height of their powers, then mostly in decline. The Lampedusas were one such family: they lived in a mansion which they maintained by occasionally opening it up to the public.

The Corberas of Salina in *The Leopard* are imbued with barely disguised autobiographical elements from Lampedusa's own idealized family history. Giulio Fabrizio Tomasi, the author's great-grandfather, was an amateur astronomer, a quiet man, notwithstanding his fits of temper, a little bigoted, with a few peculiar idiosyncrasies such as an inclination for science, but really altogether unexceptional. His son, Giuseppe Tomasi, the author's grandfather, wrote in his *Journal* that his father's villa mostly saw the comings and goings of the clergy, and hardly any social life. The family as he depicted it seems without any real ambition, and is a far cry from the fictional description of their descendant: there is nothing of the awesome patriarch in Giulio, who keeps himself at a distance from worldly pleasures and the world at large. His scientific gifts are also exaggerated in the novel – he had made no discoveries and was unrecognized in the scientific world, though his scientific library, mostly in French, was up to date.

The Lampedusas' reputation had been established by a single member of the Tomasi family – Prince Ferdinando Maria, who was mayor of Palermo in the mid-eighteenth century, and who brought the family to the fore of social and political life. Lampedusa's parents – Giulio Tomasi, Duke of Palma, and his wife Beatrice Tasca di Cutò – had themselves great expectations, and Beatrice's dowry was large enough to warrant their ambitions. Beatrice was very much an unconventional product of Palermitan aristocracy. Her liberal education and wide reading set her apart: her influence on her son would be huge, and later cause no end of conflict with his wife, as the two women clashed over their claim on him. Beatrice encouraged and directed Lampedusa's cultural interests; they also travelled extensively together. His father, on the other hand, seemed to him cold and distant: Lampedusa felt rejected, and this marked him greatly.

Lampedusa's great-grandfather on his mother's side, Alessandro Filangeri di Cutò, married a Milanese singer, Teresa Merli Clerici, after the death of his first wife, and had only one legitimate heir, his daughter Giovanna, the author's grandmother. When Alessandro died in 1854, Giovanna was only four years old. Her tutor deemed it best to remove her and her mother from the unpleasant situation in Sicily, as her father's legacy was fought over, so Giovanna grew up and was educated in Paris. She only returned to Sicily in 1867, in order to marry Lucio Tasca d'Almerita, the heir to a recent fortune. She had five daughters: Beatrice (Lampedusa's mother), Teresa (m. Piccolo), Nicoletta (also known as Lina, m. Cianciafara), Giulia (m. Trigona di Sant'Elia) and Maria, who never married

and eventually committed suicide. The five Cutò sisters –
beautiful, rich, uninhibited and more educated than the
average – also carried on part of their mother's eccentricity.

Giuseppe's aunt Lina died in the great Messina earthquake of 28th December 1908. Only three years later, her
sister Giulia was murdered by her lover, Vincenzo Paternò
del Cugno, who then tried to shoot himself, but survived
and was tried in Rome in 1912. This trial greatly affected
the family, not least because the defence made a point of
the shamelessness of the Cutò sisters, with their liberal
education and idiosyncratic upbringing. Maria suffered
greatly – as did Beatrice. As a result, Lampedusa's parents
retired from the public eye, and the family home was closed
to visitors and strangers.

Lampedusa was then sixteen. He completed secondary school at the Liceo Garibaldi in Palermo, getting his
diploma in 1914. The following year, he enrolled at the
University of Rome to study Law. His parents probably
hoped he would follow in the footsteps of his uncle Pietro,
a diplomat and in those days Italian plenipotentiary to the
King of Bavaria – but Lampedusa never sat a single exam,
either at the time or after the war, when he re-enrolled at
the University of Genoa. In November 1915, he was called
to arms, and signed up for an exclusive fast-track military
training which allowed young men from good families to
become auxiliary officers. He trained in Messina, and
was appointed Corporal in May and assigned to a battery
stationed in Augusta, under the command of Lieutenant
Enrico Cardile, a man of letters with whom he became
good friends. In 1917, Lampedusa trained at the Military
Academy in Turin to become an officer, and was sent to the
front in September, just a month before the famous Battle
of Caporetto (24th October–19th November 1917), which

was one of the greatest military defeats in Italian history. The Italian army suffered huge losses as they were pushed into retreat under the assault of the Austro-Hungarian forces. Lampedusa had been assigned to an artillery observation point on the slopes of Mount Asiago. As the enemy advanced, his station was cut off, and he was captured and taken prisoner by a company of Bosnian soldiers.

Not much is known about his time as a prisoner – Lampedusa was never very talkative about his private life, and said very little about this particular period. There are however a few memorable anecdotes, such as the time he allegedly went on a night-time tour of Vienna, which included a visit to the Opera, dressed up as an Austrian officer, having agreed with the real Austrian officer accompanying him that he would not attempt to escape, but refusing to give his word on it; or the time he did escape from Szómbathely, a prison camp in Hungary, again dressed as an Austrian officer, only to be apprehended at the Swiss border and threatened with the death penalty for desertion, until somebody realized he was an Italian prisoner of war in disguise.

Eventually, with the collapse of the Austro-Hungarian Empire, Lampedusa did manage to escape, and returned to Italy on foot about a year after he was taken prisoner. In 1919, he was once more serving his country in Casale Monferrato in the Piedmont region as a public-security officer dealing with the disturbances of the post-war period. He was finally dismissed in February 1920, after becoming a lieutenant.

Little is known about his childhood friends or the aftermath of war, but there is no doubt that Lampedusa's love of literature was firmly established during this period. Alongside his friends Fulco Santostefano della Verdura and Lucio Piccolo, who was also his cousin, he read widely and avidly. Fulco introduced him to the great French poets – from Mallarmé to Verlaine and Valéry. Lampedusa had learnt French from his mother, and always maintained that he was fluent in German, which had been an essential part of his and his cousins' early education. However, although he admired German literature, he would never be passionate about it. His alleged fluency was really wishful thinking on his part: his German was poor, and no Austrian would have believed it was his mother tongue. The Viennese tour in disguise was probably just a figment of his imagination. Shortly after the end of the war and his imprisonment, he immersed himself in English literature. There are several copies of English classics in the Lampedusa library which date from between 1919 and 1922 and are signed "Giuseppe Tomasi di Palma". These must have been years of intense reading – years during which he became acquainted with Shakespeare, Coleridge, Trollope and Joyce among others, and the time when Lucio Piccolo dubbed him "the Monster", on account of his voracious reading habits.

At around the same time, Lampedusa suffered a serious nervous breakdown, and there were rumours that he was sexually impotent. He tried to get away from Palermo as much as possible: he regularly travelled around Italy with his mother, and often stayed with three comrades from his prison-camp days, who remained among his best friends. One of them, Massimo Erede, introduced him to Mario Maria Martini, the editor of a distinguished literary magazine.

Lampedusa's diplomat uncle, Pietro Tomasi della Torretta, had in the meantime left Bavaria to return to Russia, where he had been at the start of his career. During his time in St Petersburg between 1899 and 1903, he had met Baroness Alice Wolff, née Barbi. She was the daughter of an Italian musician who had made a name for himself in Germany, and she herself had studied the violin, and then begun a highly successful concert career as a mezzo-soprano, becoming one of Brahms's favourite Lieder singers and possibly his mistress. In 1893, however, at the age of thirty-five, Alice Barbi abandoned her singing career and married Boris Wolff, a Baltic baron, with whom she had two daughters – Alessandra, born in 1894, and Olga, born in 1896.

Boris Wolff died in 1917, and in 1920 Pietro Tomasi married Alice, who was fifteen years his senior, and thus sardonically referred to as "the young Alice" by her sister-in-law Beatrice in her correspondence with her son. In 1922, after having been Minister of Foreign Affairs and Senator of the Kingdom, Tomasi della Torretta was appointed Italian Ambassador in London, where he stayed until 1927, when he was removed because of his disagreements with the Fascist regime. In 1925, his nephew Giuseppe went to visit him. This would be the first of many trips to Britain.

During his several long-term stays in Britain, Lampedusa set out to reconcile the landscapes of his literary imagination with reality. His spoken English was awkward at best and, for all his reading, he had little actual experience of the world, preferring a novelistic take on life. Lampedusa travelled all over Britain – allegedly even getting engaged in Scotland. He would wander the streets of London searching for the city Dickens described, visit the places evoked by an author in order to relive his works, and even assert that a few verses from Burns were a foolproof method of courting girls. It should be noted that Lampedusa's Britain was very much that of his own social class: he had no contact with the working classes, nor was he interested in the most parochial aspects of British life. Nevertheless, England would remain Lampedusa's ideal country.

Lampedusa travelled to Britain in 1925, 1926 and 1927, and again in 1928 and 1931, though by then he could no longer count on his uncle's hospitality, and his own fortunes had taken a turn for the worse. During his first trip to London in 1925, he had met Alessandra Wolff, also known as "Licy", the eldest daughter of his uncle's wife. She later said, of their first meeting, that having been left to their own devices by her parents, they headed towards Whitechapel talking about Shakespeare. Certainly their shared love of literature was an important factor in their relationship: both of them seemed to be people who had turned to literature as an escape from their inadequacy for real life.

Licy, however, was married, though at the time of that first meeting she was already separated from her husband, the Baron André Pilar, whom she had wed in 1918. One of the few tsarist officers to have survived the Battles of the Masurian Lakes, he spent most of his time between Riga and Germany in the Twenties. His marriage with Licy had been unhappy. Pilar was rumoured to be homosexual, and the early days of their union were tempestuous. As a result, Licy suffered a nervous breakdown, which was treated with insulin and, later, with psychoanalysis by Julius Felix Boehm, a pupil of Karl Abraham, the founder of the Psychoanalytical Society in Berlin, of Baltic origin (later Boehm was the head of the Goring Institute, the Psychoanalytical Association connected to the Nazis, and became a specialist in the treatment of homosexuals, many of whom he sentenced to death). This was Licy's first experience of psychoanalysis, which was to become her life's profession.

In later years, Licy claimed that it had been love at first sight between her and Lampedusa. Their surviving correspondence, however, suggests otherwise. Licy also claimed that Lampedusa visited her at Stomersee, the Wolffs' estate near the Latvian border with Estonia and Russia, two years after their first meeting in London. In fact, he appears to have made his first visit only in August 1930. That same year, the couple also met in Rome, where she was visiting her mother at his uncle's house in Via Brenta. Their romance developed quickly. Madly in love, Lampedusa sent her daily love letters full of Proustian reminiscences. In January 1932, while she was staying with her mother in Rome, Licy was invited to spend Easter in Palermo. They had decided to get married, and though their families had not been informed, they were certainly suspicious. In the meantime, Licy had obtained a divorce from Pilar, and Lampedusa had gathered all the necessary paperwork. They married in Riga on 24th August 1932.

On that same day, Lampedusa wrote to his parents announcing his decision. Naturally reserved and keen to avoid confrontation, he hoped to receive a congratulatory telegram, but five days later, having obtained no response, he sent an agonized letter to his mother. Licy, on the other hand, proved to be rather more independent from parental influence. Her family, who were also informed of the marriage as a fait accompli, immediately sent her their congratulations. Her mother's many questions, on the other hand, remained unanswered.

Eventually, both families met the couple in Bolzano in October. During this meeting, the signs of all future tensions were already evident. Beatrice had no intention of parting from her son, and opposed their plans to live in a separate apartment, while Licy insisted on their independence. Predictably, settling in Palermo proved difficult, and Licy soon returned to her Baltic estate. Lampedusa joined her in the summer and stayed well into the winter, then returned to Sicily for Christmas and tried to convince her to join him, but Licy refused with a harsh letter.

Things did not improve with the death of Lampedusa's father in 1934. In fact, the author was forced to stay even longer in Palermo to take care of the ongoing inheritance squabbles. The days of his European wanderings were over, and the couple remained apart, meeting a couple of times a year: eventually at Stomersee in the summer, in Rome for Christmas, and occasionally for shorter periods in Palermo. Licy's letters outnumber Lampedusa's. During those years she was often sick and presumably a hypochondriac. In 1936, Licy spent a long time in Italy, in order to become a member of the Italian Psychoanalytic Society. She was admitted without an exam, on the strength of a report on two clinical cases which had greatly impressed Edoardo Weiss, who had trained in Vienna in the Freudian circle and was then president of the society.

The couple's relationship was almost entirely epistolary. The long letters travelling back and forth from Latvia to Palermo generally avoided any topic that might cause friction: they included minute accounts of their diets, extensive commentaries and observations on their beloved dogs, travel notes and, on Lampedusa's part, detailed descriptions of encounters with mutual and approved acquaintances – though these were few and far between. Whenever the subject of resuming their life together in Palermo came up, Licy's replies were scathing, and she expressly stated that she would not bear her mother-in-law's interference.

The Second World War was devastating both for Lampedusa and for Licy, particularly because it brought the loss of their childhood homes, which had always been their refuge from the world outside. In December 1939, Lampedusa was recalled to arms. He went on a two-month refresher course and was mobilized before the war broke out, but managed to get himself discharged only three months later on account of rheumatoid arthritis in his right leg. In the meantime, after the Ribbentrop-Molotov Pact, Licy was forced to leave the Stomersee estate. She fought to save her belongings, and tried to obtain passports for some Jewish friends in Riga, but by the end of the year she had to flee to Rome. In 1941 she returned to Latvia, which had been occupied by German troops during the Siege of Leningrad. She visited Stomersee several times, sleeping in a tent. The castle had been ransacked, and the peasant population deported. She remained in Latvia until the end of 1942, when the Russian counter-offensive began.

Lampedusa displayed far less fighting spirit: he was resigned and despondent. He was once more entirely under the control of his mother, and spent most of his time with his cousins. Towards the end of 1942, both he and his mother moved in with the Piccolos at Capo d'Orlando. The Piccolos' residence was the only house where he would ever truly feel at ease after the family seat in Palermo was destroyed by the bombings. In November, Licy finally returned from Latvia, and Lampedusa joined her in Rome for Christmas, but went back to Sicily almost immediately. He was looking for a house near the Piccolos, not wanting to take further advantage of his cousins' hospitality. In 1943 he rented a house in Contrada Vina, and moved in with his mother. He frequently travelled to Palermo, constantly preoccupied with the fate of the family home in Via Lampedusa, which looked worse and worse for wear, but had yet to be directly hit.

In February, he once more tried to convince his wife to join him, but this was in vain. They continued their correspondence throughout 1943, their letters full of the horrors of the war. On 22nd March, a ship was blown up in Palermo's harbour. The debris that fell on the family home took the roof off the library room: many of the books in the Lampedusa collection still bear the traces, ingrained with soot and shrivelled with rainwater. On 5th April, the building was hit directly: Lampedusa surveyed the ruins and then headed to the villa of Stefano Lanza di Mirto in Santa Flavia on foot. He stayed there for three days, mute with shock and grief, before returning to Capo d'Orlando.

In July 1943, the rented house in Contrada Vina was also bombed while Lampedusa and his mother were out. By then, the Allied landings had started, and the coast was unsafe. Soon after, fearing a German invasion and the division of the country, Licy joined them in Capo d'Orlando, and the three moved inland to a house in Ficarra, a village in the surrounding hills, where they lived out the last days of the Allied invasion.

In mid-October, after the Armistice, the two families separated once more. It was the first time that the couple lived in Sicily on their own, without his mother. They moved to Palermo, while Beatrice remained in Ficarra. Shortly afterwards she moved into a hotel in Capo d'Orlando, where she would remain for two years. In 1946, she refused to go and live once more with her son, and moved back into a wing of the derelict family mansion on her own, where a few months later she died.

Between 1943 and 1946, Lampedusa and Licy lived in a rented room in Piazza Castelnuovo in Palermo. Times were hard: the city had been destroyed, inflation was rampant, many people were poor, homeless and living in misery. Licy threw herself into her psychoanalytic studies. She often travelled to Rome, and started practising and teaching in Palermo. Lampedusa was once again involved in the ongoing family succession feuds over the division of his great-grandfather's estate. In November 1945, an agreement was finally reached. The second floor of a building in Via Butera 42 was allotted half to Lampedusa and half to his cousin Carolina. Lampedusa moved in, though the place was in a terrible state of disrepair.

In 1950, the first and second floor of the adjoining building were put on sale. The whole building had once been the property of the Lampedusas, but in 1865 half of it had been sold to the shipbroker De Pace. Lampedusa now bought back part of the De Pace property on a mortgage. Licy had left him alone in Palermo. With a broken heart, he managed to move from his childhood home to the building in Via Butera. Throughout 1951, he dealt with co-inheritors, banks and lawyers, overseeing the necessary restoration of the building.

In the meantime, there was not enough money to pay back the mortgage, something Lampedusa would hide from his wife to his death. Yet, despite his financial troubles, some rewards awaited. In 1944 Lampedusa was selected to be the president of the provincial and eventually the regional Red Cross. He stayed in charge until 1947, fulfilling his role with zeal.

In the Fifties, Lampedusa seemed to have regained his balance: his interest in literature revived, and he was no longer dependent on his mother or his wife. Alongside some friends, he began to frequent the house of Bebbuzzo Sgadari di Lo Monaco, a music critic and great lover of culture. His home was a meeting place for all intellectuals coming through Palermo. It was here that Lampedusa and Lucio Piccolo met their third cousin, Gioacchino Lanza, who later became Lampedusa's adopted son. By 1953 they were close friends.

In 1953, Lampedusa offered to teach English language and literature to Francesco Orlando, then a law student. They started with language lessons three times a week in the living room of the first floor of Via Butera. Soon enough they moved on to literature. At the beginning of the course, Lampedusa was surrounded by a small group of followers, who attended fairly regularly up to the time when he reached Shakespeare. Then they slowly lost interest – until they all reappeared when he covered Eliot and Joyce in the summer of 1954. Between the autumn of 1953 and September 1954, Lampedusa wrote by hand about a thousand pages, which were to become his *English Literature*, finally published by Mondadori in 1990–91.

After the English course ended in 1954, Lampedusa set out to draw one up in French literature. This was never as complete as the English one, but there are nonetheless some five hundred pages in his minute handwriting. Originally, both courses had been created after Francesco Orlando had decided to abandon law in order to dedicate himself to literature. Orlando later wrote in his *Memories of Lampedusa* that the author seemed to have gradually lost interest in his relationship with his pupil. Throughout the winter and spring of 1955, he was already working on *The Leopard*.

Lampedusa may have been motivated in part from the emergence of Lucio Piccolo as a poet himself. In 1954, Lucio's mother Teresa had died, leaving Lucio free to dedicate himself to his interests. Before then his main passion had been music: he had been a talented musician, a connoisseur of Wagner, and had been composing a Magnificat for the last thirty years, though in the Thirties his musical career had come to a sort of standstill. After his mother's death, however, the verses came thick and fast, and he published a small volume at his own expense in 1954, entitled *9 liriche* (*9 Poems*). This volume was sent to Eugenio Montale, with a letter of introduction from Lampedusa, but the wrong postage was paid. Montale would later claim that he read the volume especially because he'd paid 180-lire excess to receive it. In any case, he was impressed and invited Lucio to attend a forum where established authors would introduce emerging or unknown ones. Lampedusa accompanied his cousin.

Apparently, the idea of writing a novel about his great-grandfather was one he had entertained for a long time. The original plan was to write a novel taking place over the course of twenty-four hours – just like Joyce's *Ulysses* – as attested by the first part of the novel. In June 1955 the story had already been drafted and edited several times, when Lampedusa set it aside to write 'Childhood Memories'. This work would contribute significantly to the central chapters of *The Leopard*, which thus extended beyond the scope of its Joycean roots.

Moreover, two visits to Palma di Montechiaro – the ancient feudal town of the Lampedusas – in the summer and the autumn of 1955, also proved a strong influence and inspiration. The town had been founded by twin brothers Carlo and Giulio Tomasi on 3rd May 1637, and in the following years had been imbued with familial religious zeal. Having become a duke, Carlo renounced worldly life to become a Theatine monk. The title and fiefdom went to his twin Giulio, who in 1659 bequeathed his palace to the Monastery of the Holy Rosary, where his four daughters and later his wife all took monastic vows. Giulio's firstborn, Giuseppe, followed in the footsteps of his uncle and became a Theatine; he was later sanctified. His sister Isabella, too, who had taken the name of Maria Crocifissa, was one of the great mystics of seventeenth-century Sicily.

This saintly family history was somewhat obscured by the ensuing family feuds over inheritance. Nonetheless, when Lampedusa visited Palma in August 1955 for the first time, he was extremely taken with the place. Upon his return to Palermo he enthusiastically organized a second visit along with Licy, Gioacchino Lanza and his fiancée.

On 24th May 1956, a first version of the novel, in four parts, was sent by Lucio Piccolo to Count Federici, a representative of Mondadori with whom he had been in touch. In the meantime, the novel was still developing – a new chapter was sent to Federici on 10th October. On 10th December, however, the novel, now in six parts, was rejected. Lampedusa was greatly disappointed, but writing was now his life, and he did not get discouraged.

In the last few months of his life, from the autumn of 1956 to the winter of 1957, Lampedusa wrote another two chapters of *The Leopard*. Between January and February 1957, he set down the novel on paper once more: it was now in eight parts. He also wrote, towards the end of 1956, 'Joy and the Law' and, in the winter of 1957, 'The Siren'. That same winter he also started a sequel to *The Leopard*, *The Blind Kittens*, of which we only have the first chapter.

In December 1956, the adoption of Gioacchino Lanza went through. Aside from some financial difficulties, everything seemed to be going well. In February 1957, the manuscript of *The Leopard* was sent to the novelist Elio Vittorini, who worked as an editor at Einaudi. At the same time, a patient of Licy's, Giorgio Giargia, had offered to show it to Elena Croce, the daughter of Benedetto Croce, and a lady of great cultural influence. This last contact would be the path to publication.

In April 1957, Lampedusa was diagnosed with lung cancer. Although he had suffered from a few recurring ailments, complaining especially of smoker's cough and a limp due to his rheumatism, there was no hint of his final illness until he started coughing up blood. A tumour in his right lung was found. In late May he went to Rome to have it removed, but the cancer was too far advanced. He was advised against the operation due to the state of his lungs and the position of the tumour. He tried cobalt therapy, but died on the 23rd July.

He left behind letters for both his wife and his adoptive son. In them, he asked them to pursue the publication of his novel, though he insisted it should not be at their expense. On 2nd July he had received a letter from Vittorini, who had read and in his turn rejected the novel on behalf of Einaudi, mostly on ideological grounds. In the end, *The Leopard* was published posthumously by Feltrinelli in November 1958, after Elena Croce signalled it to the novelist and editor Giorgio Bassani. The following year it won the Premio Strega, the most prestigious Italian literary award, and has since then become an international bestseller and a universally recognized twentieth-century classic.